PENGUIN METRO READS

ENCOUNTERS OF A FAT BRIDE

A marketing professional by qualification, Samah is working towards a career in storytelling. A keen enthusiast of films, fashion, food and fitness, her ultimate goal is to travel the world. She lives in Mumbai with her best friend who also happens to be her husband.

ENCOUNTERS OF A FAT BRIDE

SAMAH

Penguin
metro reads

PENGUIN METRO READS

USA | Canada | UK | Ireland | Australia
New Zealand | India | South Africa | China

Penguin Metro Reads is part of the Penguin Random House group of companies
whose addresses can be found at global.penguinrandomhouse.com

Published by Penguin Random House India Pvt. Ltd
7th Floor, Infinity Tower C, DLF Cyber City,
Gurgaon 122 002, Haryana, India

First published in Penguin Metro Reads by Penguin Random House India 2017

Copyright © Samah Visaria 2017

ISBN 9780143439998

Typeset in Sabon by Manipal Digital Systems, Manipal
Printed at Thomson Press India Ltd, New Delhi

www.penguin.co.in

To all the fat brides out there—
you're going to rock your wedding!

Prologue

'It happened in her sleep,' I overheard a woman, whom I did not immediately recognize, tell my mother. She nodded sympathetically, while I stood behind her quietly. Father had chosen not to come.

'She lived a good life. We are lucky. She celebrated ninety-four birthdays.'

'True, true,' nodded Mother. Everyone around was in a sombre mood though no one was hysterical with grief.

'Is that your daughter?' the woman said, straining her neck to look past my mother as if I were completely hidden.

'Yes, yes, this is my daughter Madhurima,' Mother said, propelling me to the front. On cue, I smiled just enough to appear polite without seeming happy. It was a funeral after all.

'My god, you've grown so big,' came her reply. Yes, I had grown at least three sizes bigger since I may have last met her but I'm sure that's not what she meant. Or maybe she did?

'Is she married?' she asked my mother as if I were mute, the fact that we were at a funeral irrelevant.

'No, not yet, we are looking for a boy. Do you have anyone in mind?' asked Mother, returning her enthusiasm. The two women launched into a detailed discussion as I slowly retreated into a corner.

The inevitable had begun.

1

About 600 days before the wedding

My first brush with wedding-dom was long before I actually got married. Family friends and relatives had started the annoying 'You're next' nudges a while ago. Post my twenty-fifth birthday, whether it was a wedding in the family or a general outing where a quorum of my family was present under one roof, the topic of my potential marriage was brought up at least once. Suddenly from being 'single', I was termed 'unmarried'. One aunt was even tactless enough to pitch her distant nephew to my mother at a family member's funeral. They must have been desperate if they were asking for my hand.

Realistically speaking, I would be no one's first choice in an arranged marriage—a fact I had accepted several birthdays ago.

You see, at 5'2", I weighed 93 kilos. Generally speaking, which boy would readily want to marry a girl like that? Especially, one he didn't even know?

So, one day, my maternal grandmother woke up with an agenda. As far back as I can remember, she had stayed with us. Legend has it that she had moved to our place to help Mother in the final weeks of her pregnancy. After I was born, no one ever felt the need for her to leave.

'Bhushan!' she summoned my father to the dining table. 'Since you have no interest in your daughter's future, I will take it upon myself to start thinking of her marriage,' she declared. Mother and I remained mute spectators.

'But we have started telling people to keep an eye out for a boy,' Father protested weakly.

'And you think a match will come along just like that? Knocking on your door? Every home we know of has at least one girl looking for a groom. No outsider is going to find a boy for your daughter. No one has the time. We need to think of other ways. I saw an advertisement of a matrimonial website in the newspaper. How about creating an account for Madhu?' Grandma suggested.

'Great idea,' said Father. 'I will set it up by the end of this week.'

'This week? Oh, forget it! I will have it set up by the afternoon itself,' Grandma said confidently. And knowing how determined she was, I didn't doubt it.

I was neither excited nor repulsed by the idea. Socially conditioned for the arranged marriage process since my cousin's recent arranged marriage, I knew I had it coming.

When you don't already have someone to marry and yet *must* get married, the alternative is finding a match either through a known source or with the help of the internet.

Word had spread among our near and dear ones but we hadn't found any suitable takers yet. In the last few weeks, my parents had realized that this was a tougher responsibility than they had reckoned, mainly because I was overweight. A matrimonial website was not the preferred route for my parents, but they felt they needed to increase the chances of finding a match. And what easier way than tricking people by hiding my largeness behind an electronic medium?

The next step—a profile of 'Kumari Madhurima Pandey' (yours truly) was craftily created on shubhshaadi.com. If my name didn't already make me sound like someone who is at least forty, then adding 'Kumari' to it surely did the trick, even though it was added to signify my singlehood.

'It's done, it's done!' declared my grandma victoriously a little after dinner that evening. Without showing much eagerness, I quietly slipped into my room and quickly logged on to the said website to check my grandmother's doing.

There were a few other profiles of the same name, surprisingly, and they were all bad, but mine surely beat them all.

Only my face, which didn't immediately give my size away, was put up in the profile picture—an obvious move. A few generic details like age and height were listed, along with a description of me that read: 'Lovely, sweet girl. Fair complexion. Big eyes, healthy figure, heavy chest, long hair. Respectful, graduate.'

I held my breath for a few seconds after reading this. I was shocked at my grandma's description of me. Her recent adeptness at using the computer was inspiring but the description infuriated me.

I refreshed the page six times to believe that the words 'heavy chest' were actually written and not a figment of my imagination. The words did not vanish and will continue to haunt me for the rest of my life.

Offended, I stormed into Grandma's room for a confrontation, but couldn't accuse her of anything because the topic was out of my comfort zone. When she eventually learned what had upset me, she laughed and patted me on the shoulder, offering advice.

She tried her best to explain that we had to highlight features and qualities of mine that would attract prospective grooms. I didn't know 'big breasts' were a quality. When I countered her, saying we would get offers from perverts, she retorted, 'Even the best and most saintly of men like big breasts.' I didn't have any rebuttal to that and was too surprised at having such a conversation with my grandmother! However, the awkwardness did not end there.

'You know your grandfather and I also got married via a newspaper ad,' she said proudly. Of course, I knew that! It was a well-known and oft-repeated tale in my family. The newspaper ad route used to be the most common one in that era.

'Do you know what his newspaper ad said?'

Even if I had known, I was expected to say 'no', so I obediently obliged.

'Well, one of the requirements listed in your grandfather's ad was that the bride must be big busted,' Grandma said, blushing. My jaw dropped. Had I heard it right?

The anecdote came as a shock, hilarious to an extent and disturbing to another. Grandma was looking nostalgically at grandfather's photo on the wall as if this was something to remember him fondly for. It was, well, creepy, to say the least.

My late grandfather was a well-known scholar of his time. I could never have imagined this side of his personality. Grandma said it was not uncommon for men to ask for well-endowed brides. In fact, mothers and sons of her time discussed such things with ease. I didn't know what to make of this, but didn't dwell on it much.

After the discussion with my grandmother, I went back to my room to take another look at my profile but could not overcome the disastrous and misleading description. If all my swollen-looking body parts had to be mentioned, then my nose, arms, stomach, hips, thighs, fingers and toes ought to be on the list too.

That night I could not sleep. And the next day I woke up with new-found motivation to pursue higher studies, preferably away from Gurgaon, (it wasn't rechristened then) where we lived.

The next day during lunch, I tactfully put forth an idea at the dining table.

'Do you remember Dipti from my college?' I asked nonchalantly. There was no Dipti in my college but it didn't matter. Everyone pretended to remember my fictitious friend anyway.

'I bumped into her the other day. She has just finished her MBA. Says her job prospects are doubling by the day. I was also thinking of doing an MBA,' I lied. I'd had no intentions of studying further until the previous day.

Quietly, I dipped my spoon into a bowl of curd, avoiding my grandmother's eyes, but sensing she could see through my move.

'Great idea,' Father said proudly and that was it. I licked the spoon victoriously as Grandma's face broke into a knowing smile.

So while many of my girlfriends had decided to drop the idea of an MBA in order to get married, I decided to pursue an MBA so that my parents would drop the idea of marriage.

A year or two away would do me well, I thought, though nothing would ever eradicate 'heavy chest' from my memory.

2

545 days before the wedding

Several weeks had passed since I 'successfully' brought down what could have been the weirdest profile on any matrimonial website. Yes! I had thrown a fit; I had sworn never to marry if my profile on shubhshaadi.com was not taken down the very next day after it was created.

But it wasn't much later that I realized that my success in dodging the bullet was more temporary than I had imagined.

Initially, everyone at home was surprised by my sudden decision to do an MBA. They had played it smart by supporting my plans of studying further, Grandma included, but their traditionalism had eventually resurfaced when they laid down the condition that I do any one-year-long course from the city itself.

My family is stuck in an identity crisis. They want all the praises and credit for being a modern family, but their old-fashioned ways often catch up with them.

Luckily, I wasn't hell-bent on an MBA abroad. I wanted to study further for the sake of prolonging my singlehood. In a way, it was better for me to study in Gurgaon because I could then keep my job as a sales executive at ACM Motors. I had landed the job after graduating from Pearl University four years ago. But I didn't tell my parents about this plan. I took full credit for sacrificing my wish for theirs. I eventually settled for a part-time MBA course at a college nearby and managing that with work meant I was doubly busy.

Everyone at home could see that I had no time to spare those days. I thought I had silenced them on the marriage front, for a while at least, until I overheard them one day when I returned home earlier than usual. It was the middle of the week. I was supposed to have an evening lecture, which was called off at the last minute because my professor had contracted diarrhoea. He suffered the verbal kind perpetually.

I let myself into the house with my set of keys. It was abnormally quiet in the living area for that time of the evening. Unsuspectingly, I filled myself a glass of water from the kitchen and sipped it as I walked towards my room. The silence of the house was broken by muffled voices behind closed doors. I stepped towards the source of the voices with the stealth of a cat.

'We cannot meet them without her knowledge,' I heard my father say. Carefully, I stuck my ear to the shut door.

'It is just a meeting, baba. Why are you worrying so much? Think of it as a meeting with a friend,' Grandma chipped in.

So, that's what it was! They were back to setting me up. I thought of barging in and confronting them at once but I stood glued to my spot, eavesdropping further.

'He is not our friend, Ma. We all know the meeting is not casual. Everyone in the community knows he is in debt.' Debt? My mind was racing. Who were they talking about?

'Good people also suffer losses. I'm sure they are nice.'

'What if we cannot meet their demands?'

Debt? Demands? What the hell was going on? By now my interest was piqued.

'Then we will know that the match cannot be arranged,' Grandma countered. Such a mastermind she was, with an answer to everything.

'But where is the guarantee that they will keep her happy once their financial issue is taken care of?'

'There's no guarantee at all, Bhushan. Madhu will have to win their hearts too.'

Oh god! I had to win hearts? It was probably tougher than losing weight. The matchmaking was still going on in full swing, I realized. There was almost a year's time till I finished my course but that hadn't halted the hunt for my groom.

Suddenly, I needed to spew out the water I had just downed. I wanted to scream at the so-called 'adults' in my family. Even my mother was in on this! Why were they so desperate? I couldn't bear it any more. Surreptitiously, I went outside the house again.

Pretending that I was just returning home, I rang the doorbell with more force than was required. Mother let me in. Once inside, I conducted myself as nonchalantly as possible.

The three of them pretended as though there was nothing out of the ordinary. I put on a poker face as well. I had figured out that they were talking to some family from our community that was in financial distress. My father would compensate for my extra weight by paying off their debts and in return, they would accept me as their daughter-in-law.

I was devastated. Did the burden of my weight mean that I would have to 'buy' myself a groom? Did being fat mean that my family would have to pay someone to marry me? How different was this from dowry? And what if I didn't like the boy? Would I have the option of saying 'no' once they said 'yes'? With a lot of difficulty, I managed to keep my tears in check. I didn't want to cry in front of them. A part of me would not believe that my parents would ever force me to marry someone. But a part of me was frightened at the thought of this indebted family.

I walked into my room after lying that I was exceptionally tired and feeling unwell. Grandma suggested I take a nap and I agreed.

Once inside my room, I bolted the door and, with tearful eyes, jumped on the bed like a typical, distressed Hindi film heroine. The bed shook under my weight. Real life problems, I tell you!

That night I did not sleep well. My mind had gone into overdrive. I wanted to confront my family about this new plan. But I eventually decided that I would not bring up the topic at all. After all, according to them I didn't know about it. So unless they came up to me with the subject, I would pretend that I knew nothing at all. Who knew how it would turn out? Maybe they would never speak to me about it. Maybe that family wouldn't want our money. Maybe the guy would turn out to be fantastic. Maybe I would wake up weighing fifty-five kilos. Anything could happen.

I decided to wait and see what was in store.

3

539 days before the wedding

It was close to EOD at work when I got a call from Anu, my closest friend from my schooldays. I had few friends and an almost non-existent social life. All my friends were girls (convent school and being overweight are a disastrous combination. One keeps you away from boys, the other keeps boys away from you). Some of my friends were from the colony I resided in, some from school, whom I was still in touch with, some from college and some from work. I also had a few male acquaintances from work.

'Madhu, come home as soon as possible,' Anu said excitedly. It seemed like an emergency call but not a panic-stricken one. More like a call of good news.

'Okay, but what's happening?'

'IT is finally happening, Madhu! It's happening,' Anu cried. The call was a refreshing change on a mundane day at work.

Now, my girlfriends and I were all at that age and at that phase of our lives where marriage, wedding jewellery and hairstyles, bridal clothes, boys in general, potential matches and relationships, were a part of our regular chats. I, however, was an exception in such chats. I was the last to add anything worthwhile to such topics and mainly only received updates. Someone had just been engaged. Someone had just had a one-night stand. Someone was looking for a boy and things like that. The topic of Anu's marriage had been going on for a while. The hunt for a groom had begun only a few weeks ago and from the minute she had decided to get married, there was a flurry of proposals.

Anu had had many suitors even in school and college. She was the epitome of perfection. She wasn't the best at anything but was good at everything. Good grades, good looks, good at sports, etc. And she was impossible to hate. The way she conducted herself endeared her to one and all. I was never jealous of her . . . until that day.

It was almost dinner time when I reached her house. There were more people there than I had expected. I knew almost all her extended family and greeted them warmly.

People were bantering all around. The vibrancy of the household made it look like a *shaadiwala ghar* already.

'Congratulations to you too, my dear girl. You're her best friend after all,' one aunt wished me. I smiled.

'Hope you're next,' she said and I kept up the smile with difficulty.

'Heard the news?' Anu's mother came and hugged me.

'Can't wait,' someone else chipped in.

'I had better start dieting,' another was heard saying. The cacophony was getting a bit overwhelming. Or maybe I was getting a little jealous.

When I finally met Anu, she darted towards me and hugged me.

'I can't believe it, I can't believe it!' Anu said repeatedly like a stuck tape in a recorder.

For the next thirty minutes, she recounted the whole story enthusiastically. Anu Sharma was getting married to Akshay Arora. The latter was from the same community as Anu's mother. Their families had met through a common friend. Akshay lived in a palatial family bungalow on Rajpur Road in New Delhi. An MBA earning an seven-digit salary, Akshay was into sports, tennis mainly and spoke four languages. He travelled extensively on work and leisure. Every alternate weekend in the city, he played golf. He loved watching movies and TV shows. He drank occasionally and did not smoke. He once had had a passing affair with a girl from his college but had been single ever since. And he was an only child. How could anyone top that?

After listening to the unbelievably perfect description of my friend's husband-to-be, I was confident and somewhat hopeful that the man would be ugly, repulsive, or at the very least funny-looking. But when Anu pulled out his picture to show me, I realized that 'the ideal man' did exist. At approximately six feet, his taut, yet not overtly muscular body did his personality justice. One look at Akshay would suffice to guess that he was into sports. Something moved in the pit of my stomach. And no, it was not the burger I had eaten for lunch. Would I ever find someone as attractive as Akshay?

I saw more than a couple of photographs of him. There was one photograph with Anu next to him. It was taken after their third or fourth 'date'.

God! They looked insanely gorgeous together. Anu herself had an impressive figure with a height of 5'6" or 5'7". Clear complexion, attractive features, long hair, long legs, a small waist and even big round breasts—the one thing that was mine!

Her engagement was fixed for the following month and she would be married within a year. She showed me a few pictures of her outfit trials for the engagement. She looked stunning in all the options, particularly in a pink and orange lehenga with a choli that had a dangerously open back. Some girls have it all.

It was close to midnight when I reached home. Despite the happy atmosphere I had just come from, my spirits took a nosedive. Once I entered my room, it was time for the dramatic jump on the bed again. I kicked my innocent blanket and comforting pillow off the bed in frustration. Hearing about Anu's wedding would only make my family take their groom-hunting efforts to the next level. I was dreading it.

That night, sleep eluded me yet again. I was incredibly happy for my friend, but terribly sad for myself. Happy that my friend was having her fancy fairy tale come true and sad that I may never have mine.

4

535 days before the wedding

'*It's over. My life is ruined!*' This was the text message I received from Anu first thing in the morning. Groggily, still adjusting to the sunlight flooding in through the windows, I sat up straight in bed. Was the wedding off? Was the wedding with Mr Perfect off? Was he not Mr Perfect after all? The possibility interested me. What is it about seeing drama in other people's lives that makes it so fascinating?

'*What happened???????*' I replied. The extra question marks conveying the level of my concern. Two minutes later, she sent me a photograph of her eyebrows. It was obvious. Just like I had warned her, the risk of trying out a new salon had not paid off. The beautician had clearly made the right eyebrow too thin compared to the left. This meant that the left one would have to be thinned down as well. What a disaster! I immediately called Anu to offer my condolences.

* * *

It was another day of no lectures and I was home sometime between 6 and 7 p.m. after work. Those days my electronic chats with Anu were constant and more frequent than otherwise. She always had some updates or needed my suggestions regarding her upcoming nuptials. From the wedding venue and the guest list to more important things like the shape of her eyebrows, we discussed everything.

Going through the process of planning her wedding with her was bittersweet, but I decided not to let it affect me—she was my closest friend after all. And who knew, maybe I would become super-hot closer to Anu's wedding and some handsome hunk would fall head over heels for me at the functions. (Spoiler alert—that doesn't happen.)

As I let myself into the house, I saw Mother and Grandma perched on the sofa, discussing something with the TV on mute in the background. Before I could say 'Hi', Father walked into the living area from his room and exchanged a glance with my mother, as if to say, 'Should we start the discussion?' It gave me the creeps.

I hurriedly tried to flee and had almost made it to my room, when I was asked to freshen up and come to the dining table for 'a little chat'.

My mind started to race. Would this be about the indebted family? Had they agreed upon an arrangement? Was I buying a husband???

Pushing aside all negative thoughts, I speedily freshened up and came to the dining room, eager to get this over and done with. My parents and Grandma were already sitting in their usual spots. A deafening silence prevailed for a few seconds and then the inevitable began again.

'Madhu, we have been talking about finding a match for you to a few people for some weeks now,' my father started.

I had just a few seconds to decide whether to play along or to reveal that I knew about the secret groom-hunting. I decided upon the former.

'Oh? I thought we had decided that I was still studying. That we would consider marriage next year. How could you do this without telling me?' I gave my best shot at acting. My tone was agitated and higher than usual, my expression wounded. Heavy breathing followed.

Grandma retorted, 'We are fine with your studying for as long as you want. But everything else must also go along simultaneously in life. That is what gives one a perfect balance.'

'But what is the hurry? I am only twenty-five.'

'At your age I was . . .'

'Oh please, *Nani*!' I cut her off. It was high time. 'Don't give me that. I'm sure at my age you were already a mother of thirty children! Times have changed. Keep up!' I said, unleashing the irritation I felt within.

'Madhurima! You will not speak to your grandmother like that,' my mother said firmly. Within seconds, the atmosphere in the house had heated up.

'She is right, Rima,' Grandma told my mother with mock self-pity. 'Times have changed, indeed.'

'So you agree that we can wait a little longer?' I was in no mood to humour anybody.

'No, Madhu. We have just started looking for a boy. Do you know how long it could possibly take to find one?'

Everyone else was quiet. Grandma continued, 'You heard the latest about Deepa's daughter, Ragini?'

Ragini is my second cousin. The maternal family's favourite. Every teacher's pet, every girlfriend's threat. Little-Miss-Who-Eats-Everything-But-Is-Somehow-Still-Skinny Ragini. Damn her!

'Ragini has done her MBA from the best college in Mumbai. You have seen her photographs. She is prettier than top heroines. Yet, not one suitable boy could be found for her in the past eight months.'

'Oh yes, and if no boy could be found for Little-Miss-Perfect Ragini then what chance does fat old Madhu have, right?'

'Enough!' Mother intervened.

'Try to understand, Madhu,' she said in a pacifying tone. 'We are just having causal talks for now. You don't have to get married immediately. It will take us a while to find a suitable boy and then both of you will get enough time with each other before coming to a decision. But you need to be involved from the beginning. What you want, what you don't, which family is more appealing than others, everything. It will take a long time.'

'And what if you find the boy immediately?'

It was a stupid question. It wasn't as if I would say 'yes' and there would be a row of candidates under my building. Everyone remained silent.

'Fine. You people do what you want. My opinion does not matter anyway.'

'Of course, it does, *beta*,' said my father, the calmest of the lot. 'Otherwise, why would we have this discussion? We don't want to do anything without your knowledge.'

'Oh, is that so? Then why are you meeting families that are in debt? To buy a husband for me?' I said, although this was not part of my plan.

My words shocked everyone. The colour drained from their faces. Suddenly I had that edge over them, the edge that people get when they catch someone doing something wrong. My father looked away sheepishly.

'I know what you people are up to behind my back,' I said, demonstrating more offence than I actually felt. I tried my best to squeeze out a tear or two for added effect but it turned out that acting wasn't my thing, after all.

So, abandoning the discussion, I dashed into my room, bolted the door and stood with my back against it, mirroring the exact moves I had seen distressed actresses make in movies. Sliding down to the floor would have been a bit too much so I went and sat down on the bed. I stayed in my room until almost midnight, when I couldn't bear the hunger pangs any more. I hadn't caved in even when everyone came turn by turn to call me for dinner.

At about 11.45 p.m., I crept sneakily into the kitchen, where I found a covered plate of food on the counter, left most probably by Mother. Despite the current situation, the gesture made me smile and I soon found my anger melting away. After eating every edible morsel on my plate, I freshened up and then reflected on what had happened. It is amazing how a full stomach changed my mood within seconds.

The truth was although my parents hadn't kept me in the loop, they hadn't brought up the topic of the family-with-the-financial-issue with me either, probably because they didn't expect me to marry him. That had to count for something. And what did they want? They just wanted me to meet people that I approved of. It wasn't as if I was completely against marriage. I wasn't. Maybe it was worth giving this circus a shot. Slowly, I crept into my parents' room.

Mother and Father were sleeping with their backs to each other. Father was gently snoring. I knelt down beside mom and shook her lightly. 'Mumma,' I said. She woke up in a jiffy.

'What happened? Is everything okay?' she said in panic, trying to sit up.

I told her everything was fine and made her lie down again. Father was still fast asleep.

'What happened? Why are you still awake? Have you eaten?'

'Mumma, I'm ready to start looking for a boy,' I whispered. She smiled away the tears that were welling up in her eyes and embraced me.

5

528 days before the wedding

Only a few days had passed since the night I had agreed to start 'seeing boys'—whatever that meant. The decision had made everyone at home incredibly happy. The next day my father, overwhelmed and relieved to have me on board, admitted that meeting the indebted family behind my back was an unfair move. Luckily for me, that chapter was closed after the first meeting itself. The boy's family firmly believed in horoscopes and mine didn't match their son's. Sometimes, the most unexpected things can save you from tricky situations.

It all started with an unusual phone call from my grandmother during lunch hour in office.

'Hi, Nani.'

'Madhu, beta, am I disturbing you?'

'No, no. I was just about to have lunch. Is everything okay?'

'Yes. Okay, as soon as you are done eating, take a break and check your phone.'

'Okay, why?'

'I'm sending you some photographs on the Whatsup,' she said. The error made me smile but there was no point correcting her, not for the hundredth time.

'Okay, what photographs?'

'Just see them. We'll talk in the evening.'

'I have class after work.'

'Okay, then at night. Now go back to work. Bye bye.'

'Bye, Nani.'

As soon as the call was through, I rushed back from the pantry to check my phone, but there was no new message.

A few minutes later, I received a lengthy message from my ultra tech-savvy grandma.

'*Dear Madhu. I am sending you some pictures of Nishant Pandey, son of well-known family from our community. Very handsome boy. You will not have to change surname also. Ha ha. You can check him on the Facebook as well. I have met his grandmother many years ago. Rest will chat at home. Love, nani*☺☺'

I quickly downloaded the three photographs. Thin, seemingly tall, bespectacled and wearing a suit, the boy was decent-looking; the photographs, hilarious! They were professionally taken in a photo studio against different backgrounds. One was a full-length, one a mid-shot and one a close-up. Who does that! I found the whole concept lame and funny but before I could actually let out a laugh, I imagined how I would look in such photographs. Surely, worse than him by a big margin. The thought of getting such pictures taken depressed me. I would have to protest if it came to that. I generally avoided cameras, mirrors, reflective windows and anything else that reminded me of what I looked like.

Throughout my day at work and even during lectures, I kept thinking about the boy. Every time I looked at his photographs, I asked myself, 'Is he the one?' Could he be my future husband? The man I will lose my virginity to? The thought made me gag. Was I thinking too far? This was unfamiliar territory. I wondered how many men I would meet before settling down for one. Was there an average quota in the market?

After work and college, I returned home, hungry and exhausted; the upbeat atmosphere at home not in synchronization with my mood. My family was awaiting my return with enough enthusiasm on their grinning faces to tick me off. Their eagerness was directly proportional to my frustration. I wanted to go right up to them and literally give them all a good shake.

'What is it? Why are you all smiling at me like that?' I grumbled. The smiles grew wider.

'Oh, don't pretend to be coy now.'

COY? They thought I was being coy? Damn! They knew nothing of being coy then.

'If this is about the boy, please spare me.'

'Oh, don't be like that,' said Grandma. 'I'm sure you secretly liked him.'

Did I? I really didn't know.

'I'm off to bed.'

'He's coming over for tea with his family this weekend,' Mother announced softly, cautiously. At least someone was worried about my reaction.

It was time for the routine dive on to the bed. At this rate, I'd soon need a new one because the wedding circus had officially begun.

6

515 days before the wedding

Nishant Pandey's family was visiting us that evening. I could not believe that I would be doing the Tea Parade in this day and age. If anything had changed, it was the fact that I would be serving the Pandeys green tea! They were the health-conscious type. Even a fool would've known that this wouldn't have worked out. A family that had requested green tea before arrival would not welcome a ninety-three-kilo bride. But I was dolled up in a salwar kameez (which I suspect was made out of an old bedsheet) and exhibited all the same. Though reluctant, I had complied with all the dos and don'ts that the expert mothers in my house had instructed me with.

For the first ten minutes after their arrival, I was holed up in the kitchen like a rabbit in its burrow. Mother was to settle them in the living area, serve them water and then send for me when the anticipation had built up.

With shaking hands and a plastic smile, I went out to play my part. Despite the discomfort of the tummy-tucker that was trying hard (and miserably failing) to keep it all together under my outfit, Nishant's mother's eyes popped out on seeing me and mine popped out on seeing her paan-stained teeth. Health-conscious, my foot! I acknowledged them with a nod of my head and a shy smile, practised to perfection. Mother had told me to talk less. I had decided not to talk at all, unless it was absolutely unavoidable.

After the Tea Parade, I was made to sit between Nishant's sister and his mother. Ridiculous! How could I check them out while sitting next to them? Sometimes, adults don't exercise any common sense at all.

Nishant, dressed in a maroon shirt with green leaf motifs (I swear!), was soft-spoken and shy, but the same cannot be said about his family. Apart from him, his parents and younger sister, an older uncle had also come to visit us. This uncle was serving as the broker between our families. He knew my father's cousin.

Flashy, loud and unnecessarily open (and I'm not just talking about the mother's blouse), the other Pandeys didn't strike me as the ideal family on our first and only encounter. But Nishant came across as a sensible and compliant fellow, the green leaves on his shirt notwithstanding. Although I was prepared to have a five-minute, make-or-break, one-on-one chat with him on the pretext of showing him my room (Bollywood movies had trained me well), thankfully, it didn't come to that.

The whole operation lasted for about forty-five minutes. I was mainly asked about my job, daily routine and general stuff like that. I got the feeling that they had made up their mind upon seeing me. Nishant was not asked too many questions by my family. Grandma went a little overboard in praising Nishant's looks and 'vibrant style of dressing'. When they were ready to leave, Father escorted them out of the house and all the way down the building. He came back impressed with the choice of their car.

He told us that if they were interested in taking this further, in order to explore the potential between Nishant and me, then the next meeting would take place between the two of us. And if we both felt positive, then matters would officially be fixed.

As a general opinion, my father asked me what I thought about the Pandeys. I admitted to liking the boy and disliking his family.

Eventually, my opinion didn't matter because two days later when Father received their answer, it was a 'no' from their end. When he asked the middleman for a reason, he didn't cite any particular one. I wonder why Father had had to ask for a reason at all.

Wasn't it obvious?

That night we all ate in silence. Grandma, although disappointed, didn't betray her emotions. She cooked chicken biryani—her trademark dish. She rarely cooked those days, so we really looked forward to anything prepared by her. We discussed irrelevant things to no end after the meal was over.

Eventually, Grandma acknowledged the elephant in the room.

'You will face several such situations, Madhu. It is natural to get upset but try your best not to. It does not matter.'

I just managed a polite smile. One part of me wanted to wallow in self-pity, another didn't want to give a damn about someone who had rejected me. Yet another part wanted to celebrate the fact that I wouldn't have to marry Leaf Shirt and another wanted to be accepted by him and his family. I let no emotion be detected. Sometimes you have to be brave for others. Seeing me sad and embarrassed about the rejection would have been very difficult for my parents.

'Madhu will get a far better boy. That boy was too sissy,' Grandma tried once more to give us closure on the topic. 'And did you see the cut of the mother's blouse? I'm sure half of Gurgaon has seen her twins!'

'Mummy, enough,' my mother admonished her mother.

She came around the table to where I was sitting and gave me a loving hug.

'Goodnight, my princess,' she said before retiring to her bedroom.

By now, I was cranky and emotional. I wished everyone goodnight and went to bed.

Before sleeping, I silently gave myself a pep talk and prepared myself for a flurry of rejections. It had only just begun.

7

425 days before the wedding

It had been a while since the episode with the other Pandeys—my first ever rejection. Some months and many rejections later, I was particularly annoyed with my family on this particular day.

Another family had recently turned us down—me down. It had become a routine. Families of prospective husbands walked in and out of our house like it was their bathroom. Some were more obnoxious than others. They all gave varied reasons for nipping the alliance in the bud, but I knew it was invariably always the same reason.

Sometimes it irritated me no end that these families should reject me for my size. At least one woman from the boy's side, who came over for the preliminary high tea, would definitely be as big as me, if not bigger. If the boy's mother wasn't overweight, then his sister or sister-in-law definitely was. Why then was their gigantic

arse accepted and not mine? If we all are to eventually
resemble baby elephants after popping babies, then what
was the big deal if I got there a little before time?

Meanwhile, I had dropped three and a half kilos,
thanks to the diet my mother had put me on. But I guess
when you weigh so much, a few kilos off are hardly
noticeable. Often, out of frustration I ended up eating
more than I would have eaten off the diet, without my
mother's knowledge, of course. Food was my way to let
off steam. Soups and salads bored me anyway and to
have that for lunch and dinner every day while surviving
work AND college? It was hell.

My family was under a lot of stress. The topic of my
marriage was omnipresent in the house. It was like an
added member in the family. There was nowhere in the
house I could escape from it. Even when the house was
completely silent I could hear it.

I had seen Father making many calls to friends, to
friends of friends, to relatives. It always began as an
out-of-the-blue, cursory call and then, he would say,
'Okay, listen. I have something important to discuss
with you. You remember my daughter, Madhurima?'
At this point the person at the other end would either
feign to remember me or say whatever they actually
did remember of me.

'Yes, she's doing her MBA now,' he would say with
evident pride. The irony!

'Keep a lookout for her. You know, in case of any
families or boys.'

Often, there would be eligible boys within the very family of the person he was talking to and Father would be very well aware of this and yet pretend to not realize it.

I suppose the person at the other end would say something like, 'Oh, the son of my cousin's nephew's granddaughter is also looking for a girl.'

'Oh my god! I didn't think of that!' Father would say, while looking at that same boy's photograph on Facebook!

And the cycle would continue. This happened at least three times. To be fair, not all rejections were outright 'no's'. One family agreed to a second meeting. I didn't like the boy much, but what could I say to the only family that had agreed to meet me again? I thought it was worth a shot.

While I tried to be practical about it, everyone else at home got carried away.

'Oh! I knew this day would come,' Grandma exclaimed.

'They have agreed to another meeting, which means they are okay with the fact that our Madhu is on the healthy side.'

Healthy side, right! More like, unhealthy side.

'God bless them. They seem lovely, Rima. Your daughter will be very happy with them. I'm sure they'll love her nature, now that they will get to know her better.'

Mother and Father also said stuff like that, but everything went down the drain when this family too changed its stance a few days later.

Getting rejected became such a way of life that no closures were given any more. No philosophical statements about destiny, or about losing something only to be blessed with something better were made. How long can one go on harping on such nonsense that is uttered only to make oneself feel temporarily better?

So that day, I wasn't furious about the rejection. I'd somewhat come to expect it. I was furious that after another letdown my parents were still relentlessly pursuing another *rishta*. I felt like a product that needed to be sold in the marital market. I felt exposed and embarrassed. My self-confidence was eroding and the ironic part was that I didn't want to marry any of those dimwits but when the deal was off the table, I was unhappy. This way or that—there was just no relief.

'Stop it!' I yelled at the dining table. Angrily, I stood up and banged my fist on the table. Stupid move. It hurt terribly but had the desired effect. They were all taken aback, almost as if a little scared of me at that moment. I'd never before spoken like this to any of them.

'Just stop this rubbish. I had told you I was not ready and yet you people have pushed me and pushed me and pushed me. Haven't I faced enough humiliation? Aren't you all tired? Can you give this a break? I can surely use one.'

'Madhu, relax, beta,' said Grandma.

'No, I will not relax,' I banged the table once again. To be honest, it was fun. It made me feel authoritative.

'Listen to me. I understand what you are going through. But it has to be done.'

'No. It does not. You pretend to be modern and forward. It's time to show your worldly thinking. And it's not even like we have an option. I agreed to meet boys. But nobody seems to want to marry me,' I said, feeling tears prick my eyes.

'You can't say that. You think there are no fat boys in the world who want to get married? Good, nice, respectable people—all have flaws. It's just a matter of time till we find a good home.'

'So then why look at thin boys? And good boys. And rich boys. Look at ugly, short, poor boys. Oh wait! You're already doing that. And even THEY are not willing to marry me. Why are you so desperate to get rid of me?'

'Stop it, Madhu. Don't talk rubbish. And it's not as if you approved of the boys who have come along. I know that you too wanted to turn down the rishtas that have come so far.'

'But it never came to that!' I protested and paused for a moment. Something clicked in my mind. At that moment, I knew what I wanted. I wanted to be at the other end for a change. I wanted to reject somebody. I wanted to have that option. I wanted my family to know that they could not assume I would go along with any boy who did not reject me. I had my weight and my ego in equal measure. But before carrying out my revenge, I needed a break, a well-deserved one, from this topic.

'Please, Papa,' I addressed the most susceptible one in my family, one who could not refuse me easily.

'Can we give this hunting a break? I just want to be left alone for some time. Please. I'll come to you when I'm ready again. I agreed on my own earlier too, right? Just for now, stop looking so actively.'

'But, beta,' Mother intervened again.

'No "but". You can't force me.'

'We are not. Okay, we will stop looking for some time. Let's concentrate on your jogging and diet for a few days.'

Oh! Did I mention? I was being subjected to jogging too. Though in the last four weeks, Mother had managed to take me for what she calls a jog, but which is most definitely sleep-walking, only on three mornings.

'Okay,' I agreed. I'd pick jogging and eating leaves any day over meeting more boys and their families.

I slept with great ease that night, certainly more easily than I had during that entire phase. But I knew that I wouldn't be off the hook for too long.

8

380 days before the wedding

I had a day off at work so I was rather annoyed at being woken up early by Mother that day. On holidays, I loved to sleep for as long as I wanted to. Grandma didn't approve of the habit. She said it wouldn't work in my marital home. Well, it was just another reason for not getting married.

No reason was cited for the unceremonious waking up. Oddly, I was being spoilt for choice at breakfast. Instead of fruits and cereal, my mother, the kitchen tyrant, had made puri bhaji. FOR ME. It was like feeding the goat before slaughter, but I feasted anyway. I was hoping lunch would be a treat too, before the family told me which boy I would be meeting next. Sadly, I couldn't make it till lunch without being summoned.

Right after breakfast, the topic was rehashed. All along, this dry spell of no rishtas had been a boon for me.

Although I had agreed to go to my parents when I was ready again, the truth was that I had sheepishly decided to ignore the topic altogether, for as long as I could. I knew eventually they would come to it, so I enjoyed my freedom as long as it lasted.

Somewhere, deep down in me, there also lived a girl who had grown up watching cheesy Hindi movies, who had grown up seeing her parents in a happy marriage, who had grown up fantasizing about unrealistic romance. At one point, the idea of romance, love and marriage even excited me. But when reality hit home, it shattered the stupid mirage that the world of fiction had painted in my mind. I grew up to be nothing like the pretty girls in movies; my college life was nothing like the merry-go-round that books and movies depicted it to be. Boys around me were neither handsome nor interested in me. And the arranged marriage business was turning out to be nothing like the dreamy phase I had thought it might be. In my heart of hearts I, too, believed marriage was important. Maybe it was social conditioning from childhood that made this step seem compulsory but there was no doubt in my mind that I would delay it as long as possible.

'Madhu, beta,' Mother started off with caution.

'Hmm,' I said, switching channels on the television.

'Listen, no.'

'I'm listening, Ma,' I said, still looking at the TV.

'Pay attention, Madhu. This is important.'

I put down the remote, crossed my legs on the sofa and then turned to face my mother, who stood at a little distance, near the dining table.

'So, you want me to meet another boy?' I asked bluntly.

Mother was taken aback a little and hesitated before agreeing.

'Uh . . . yes . . . but only because it's a very good family.'

'Aren't they all? Why would we meet bad families?'

'You know what I mean. I've heard they are very kind and simple.'

'Tell me about the boy. If he's good-looking, thin or rich, then there's no point. They'll all find better girls than me.'

'Don't say that.'

'I don't want sympathy. I'm just being practical. Why waste everyone's time and effort?'

'Please, beta. Just let them come home this weekend. If you don't like them, we'll say "no" immediately.'

My mother's last words made my eyes gleam. I'd never known there to be a vicious side to me . . . until then. I was excited at the stupid prospect of saying NO. Sometimes the shallowest things give us much-needed gratification.

And so I let the wedding brouhaha begin again.

'Okay. I'll meet them next weekend,' I said, suddenly excited. Grandma caught a hint of the unexpected eagerness in my voice. I couldn't let my plan be revealed so I quickly sobered down.

'Why next?' asked Mother.

'One-and-only offer. Take it or leave it,' I said with deliberate indifference and went back to switching channels.

'You are too much! Fine. Next weekend.'

And suddenly I was waiting for the next prospective groom to walk into my house.

9

369 days before the wedding

With much irritation and little energy, I wiped off the gaudy lipstick that Grandma had put on me for the Tea Parade with the Tripathis. I have thin lips (of all the body parts that could have been thin!) and my grandmother had expertly applied the lipstick well outside the contours of my lips. 'It's a make-up trick,' she assured me. Of course, I was all for make-up, for *anything* that could enhance my (non-existent) beauty, but I was more picky than most about such things. I rarely felt that I could pull off edgy looks. Even when we went shopping, which wasn't often, I always tried a dozen things but liked only half of them and eventually picked up only one or two items. Ma's and Grandma's suggestions were never of any help. They felt I looked good in everything. To them, even cropped tops and miniskirts looked great on me. 'Just wear it and have fun,' Grandma would say. They didn't understand the way things were in this generation.

As I freshened up and climbed into bed, I reflected on how the evening had gone. It was the same old crap again. Shy boy, over-the-top mother, talkative father, irritating, unmarried sister. When would I finally find that 'click'? Would I at all? Of course, fat and ugly people also fall hopelessly in love and have crazy romances, don't they? When would it happen for me? Even though I had only agreed to meet this family for the opportunity to say 'no' to them, a part of me was still hopeful that maybe this family could be the one I marry into, maybe this boy was the one I could spend my life with. But the meeting went as predictably, as monotonously as any other.

There was only one thing to look forward to now. I was excited to tell Father to say 'no' to the Tripathis the next morning. It gave me pleasure to think of the reactions our relatives, people in our community and family friends would have when they learnt that *I* had turned the offer down; that *I* too had a choice, that *I* didn't think the family was good enough for me.

It was relatively early for bed, but I was ready to sleep all the same, eager for morning to arrive. I must have switched off the lights and tried to sleep for about fifteen minutes or so when unusually, there was a knock on my door.

'Madhu, beta. It's Papa. Have you gone to sleep?'

I indicated that I was awake with a few incoherent sounds.

Two minutes later, the lights in my room were switched on and Father sat on the edge of my bed, clearly in the mood for a chat. After a minute or two of small talk, he began a conversation I hadn't anticipated at all.

'So, beta, how did you find Harsh and his family?' he asked. It was an odd time and way to ask me this question, but I was eager to turn the boy down. It was obvious what their answer would be, but before I became the 'rejectee', I planned to use this opportunity to become the 'rejecter'.

'Ordinary. Quite boring actually. Harsh hardly spoke. Whatever,' I said and Father's face paled a little.

Yes, Papa. I can have a choice too. I can say 'no' too, I thought, but refrained from voicing it. I could feel my ego swelling up. My pulse quickened. This was exciting.

After a moment or two of weighing his thoughts, Father spoke again.

'I had a word with them on the phone after dinner,' he said softly. And my heart almost stopped. Multiple thoughts crossed my mind in a flash. Why did they call? So soon? What did they discuss? Have they already rejected me? Have I missed the opportunity? How can Fate take even this away from me? My plan was falling flat.

'Why did they call? I hope you didn't encourage anything. I hope you said that it's a "no" from me,' I said quickly, in order to save face at least in front of my father.

His expression remained grave.

'I didn't. I thought you liked them.'

I leapt out of the bed in frustration. 'Why! Why do you always have to assume! I wanted everyone to know that it was a "no" from me! Not from them! I have rejected them. They have not rejected me!' I said furiously.

'But they have not rejected you at all, beta. They liked you. They want to meet again. Soon,' said my father and that's where everything changed.

10

368 days before the wedding

I was on the verge of insomnia those days. The night Father told me that Harsh Tripathi's family was interested in meeting again, I didn't sleep. Even the following day passed deep in thought.

I had been so sure of rejecting Harsh and it had nothing to do with him. This had become a game for me. Before they could say 'no', I was prepared to fling my refusal in their faces. But that's the irony of life, it plays its trump card just when you think the game is over.

I didn't want to admit it, but it was true that their positive response greatly affected my stand on the matter. It made me unsure of my refusal and I hated myself for this. It made me think again. Why was I rejecting Harsh exactly? I didn't go gaga over him, but I didn't despise him either. Actually, I just didn't know him well enough to decide whether I liked him or not. How can one know in just one meeting? He wasn't repulsive enough for me to turn him down so soon. He deserved a second shot, a second thought, especially because he thought that I deserved it too.

I remember skipping lunch the next afternoon. The situation had killed my appetite. Shocking, I know! I browsed through his images on my phone again and again. His looks (or the lack of it) didn't bother me much. He was the shiest of the lot I had encountered so far.

I could accept his shyness. I could understand that he was thirty and still unmarried. I could understand everything suspicious about him but I couldn't wrap my head around the fact that he would want to take this further. With me? Lack of confidence in oneself can make one doubt even the best people.

Throughout my day at work, I was hyperventilating. My mind was filled with varied suspicious possibilities. Was he being forced to get married? Because he was gay? They knew we weren't filthy rich so money was not likely to be the motive. Was he impotent? And was that why he was agreeing to marry me? The impotency angle really frightened me. Fat girls also dream of macho guys, crazy sex and mind-blasting orgasms. I hadn't even kissed a boy yet.

Unfortunately, even the happiness of getting a positive response from a seemingly nice family turned bittersweet because I suspected major fishy business behind their decision to meet me again.

It's amazing how Harsh's acceptance (well, sort of) of me greatly changed my mind about him. Some of us are so hungry for love and acceptance that we automatically love and accept the ones who give it to us. I took my time to agreeing to see him, one-on-one this time, but I'm sure everyone at home already knew that I would meet him again.

That night there were waterworks at home again. Ma and Grandma had not learnt their lesson from being overexcited the first time. Nothing could be done about them. They were incurable emotional fools. I was nervous like I had never been before. Absurd as it was, this would be my first date with a boy. At twenty-five. Yes.

With an evident bounce in his voice, Father rang up the Tripathis to let them know of my go-ahead. He made the call from the living area and I stood next to the door of my room and listened carefully. Their conversation appeared to be normal, which was a relief, until I heard a disappointed 'Oh' escape my father's lips. The entire house became deathly quiet. Mother clutched the armrest of the sofa. My palms grew moist with sweat. Even my usually unfazed grandma was nervous. Who would have thought it was possible?

I told myself not to imagine the worst. No, they could not have changed their mind. I kept repeating this in my head. Father's voice became fainter as my thoughts grew louder.

'No, problem,' I heard him say and my heart sank a little more but I tried to be positive.

'Lightning never strikes the same place twice,' I told myself aloud. I didn't want to eavesdrop further so I shut the door tightly and lay down on my bed. Gently this time. The dramatic jumps had been missing from my life for a while. Would they be making a comeback?

A few minutes later, there was a knock on my door. Mother, Grandma and Father walked in. They didn't seem particularly tense. I sat up and played it cool despite the urgency of my curiosity.

It turned out that Harsh was going to be out of the country on business for the next few days. Ten to be precise. He was a tech guy who dealt in computer hardware and often travelled abroad for trade exhibitions. That's all I knew of his profession.

It was a relief that THAT was the disappointing news Father had to convey, but once I was alone, the anxiety only grew. A lot could go wrong in the coming ten days. He could change his mind on his trip to Germany. He could find a skinny girl and fall in love with her during the trip. Of course, he could change his mind even if he weren't going, but the ten-day gap and distance made me fret. I wanted to meet him soon, to seal the deal or break it, or at least move forward in some direction. Hanging in the middle just made things too uncertain and unpredictable. In a way, knowing it was a 'no' was better than this. It scared me to believe that there was a chance of finding my fairy tale come true only to have the dream snatched away. No one but I would ever understand the emotions I felt, the thoughts I reflected upon, the things I imagined in that phase.

The night ended on a happy note for a change. Putting aside negative thoughts, I deliberately thought of Harsh. He hadn't given me much to think about but I replayed that evening he visited my house again and again in my head and sometime while doing that, I fell into a peaceful sleep.

11

356 days before the wedding

Ten days later, Harsh returned from his big-shot business trip. His family was of modest means but his academic accomplishments had been a game-changer. With an impressive MBA, Harsh had got a handsome pay package for his first job at an IT firm. A few years later, he and his colleague left the firm to start their own venture. Apart from hardware, they also dealt in software solutions. Of course, I got to know all this much later in our story. Back then all I knew was that he was in the city again and I was to meet him for coffee that evening.

I planned to take a half-day at work, but ended up taking the entire day off thanks to my overenthusiastic mother and control-freak grandmother. They had an instruction for everything, from what I would wear to what I would say and eat at the coffee shop, swiftly turning my anxiety into a panic attack. While I was on the verge of vomiting due to nervousness, a massive debate was on in my bedroom over the effect of the colour red on my skin tone.

'Look how beautiful the colour is looking on her, mummy. She looks like a bride already,' my mother said to her mother holding against my face a red dress she had bought for me recently despite my protests.

'That's exactly what we want to avoid. Don't scare the poor boy away. I think she needs to wear black. It makes her look thin and tall like a model,' Grandma offered her expert advice. Considering Grandma's love for magazines, her knowledge of what a conventional model looked like was rather poor.

'But black is so dull. She should wear a red dress. There should be vibrancy in her appearance.'

'No. She should wear a black T-shirt and jeans with bright red lipstick and red heels.'

I had to intervene at this point.

'I don't own red lipstick or red heels,' I managed to pipe in, but why would a fact like that deter their heated discussion? There's no space for logic when mothers argue.

Ignoring them, I started to get ready as per my own idea of what I should wear for coffee in the middle of a bright and sunny day.

I wondered if Anu had had to go through so much preparation for her initial meetings with Akshay. Did her mother have to sit and decide what she should wear and how she should be? Surely not. But she was in a different league altogether. She didn't need to be told what to do with a boy on a date, how to speak, how to behave in order to seem appealing and desirable. Anu owned such things. She could open a coaching class or two. And the best part was that she didn't try too hard. She was a natural. Confidence exuded from every inch of her. If only it could cover a fraction of all my inches. Sigh!

Father had told me to meet Harsh at 5 p.m. at Coffee & Co. It was a well-known cafe in our area but a little far away for Harsh, who stayed on the other end of the town.

At 4.30 p.m., I was ready to leave. Mother and Grandma stood at the door, sulking over my rather 'simple' attire of jeans and a t-shirt.

'Nothing is matching,' Mother complained sorrowfully. My mother does not understand the concept of contrast, she never has. In all my childhood photographs, if you see an object with a burst of a single colour from top to bottom, you will know that that object is me. Painful memories.

Just as I was about to leave, Mother asked me to wait. She rushed into the kitchen and came back with a spoonful of curd. I consumed it obediently. I felt like I was in school again, appearing for an exam—only worse.

'I'll get the car,' Father said and left. He was going to drop me and would pick me up as well. For a date. To fix my wedding. Yes.

'Have fun,' Mother said and sent me off with a peck on the cheek.

'Try not to laugh like a hyena,' Grandma said and I countered her advice right then. She's funny once you stop taking offence at her constant jibber-jabber.

I was jittery and restless all along the way. How badly would this date go? I had no idea what to expect. What if Harsh asked me whether I was a virgin? Should I be honest? Or should I be a schmuck and pretend that I'd done it with my boss? Or should I be vague and ask him in turn? Eventually I decided that I'd just throw my coffee in his face and leave if he asked me that. (Spoiler alert— that doesn't happen).

As soon as I got out of the car, I couldn't wait to get back, back into my house, into my pyjamas and into my comfort zone. But it had to be done, so I put my apprehensions aside and walked towards my date with a smile on my face.

Once I entered the coffee shop, I quickly scanned the area only to find that Harsh hadn't reached yet. I had his phone number but decided to wait. I could tame my rebellious hair and look a little less like a lioness on the loose before he arrived. I made a hasty visit to the washroom, wiped off the obvious layer of lipstick only enough to make it look like I had 'naturally' pink lips. Someone tried to open the washroom door and my heart jumped in the typical way that the heart jumps when people try to walk in on you in the washroom, but luckily I had locked it. I brushed my hair twice to domesticate the bush it had become but it was of no use. When I came out of the washroom, I saw a man nervously fixing his hair in front of the mirror outside. It took a moment to realize that it was Harsh. We both looked at each other and burst out laughing. It was a good ice-breaker.

As we settled into our seats at a corner table, we first ordered our drinks and then began talking (by talking I mean that I spoke and he nodded from time to time). The little he spoke was about his work. I cracked a few nervous jokes that didn't deserve a single chuckle but Harsh laughed goofily on one or two occasions. His slightly crooked nose wrinkled whenever he laughed. His almond-shaped eyes looked here and there. The top two buttons of his shirt were undone. Chest hair threatened to jump out of it. It was distracting, not in a good way. He sat with his arms crossed like a stubborn kid throwing a tantrum but his polite smile was endearing. He seemed encouraging and sweet but still quite shy. I had to make most of the effort to talk and start new topics of conversation.

Harsh didn't strike me as very outgoing. While that may have been a negative aspect about him, there was also something simple about his nature (and his nerdy laughter) that appealed to me. Some of my doubts were cleared in the first meeting. I reckoned he wasn't gay. Somehow you can just tell. About the other angles, I would still have to see. We spoke nothing about marriage or the future and that was a relief.

I tried to imagine how we must have looked to passers-by. When I was in school I would look at all those couples who went on dates to coffee shops. The boys were dreamy, handsome, so much older than me that they would give me that 'oh, what a sweet baby' look. I hated it. I wanted them to look at me the way they looked at their dates. Cracking jokes, laughing more than necessary and being charming. I learned later that that was called flirting. And the girls! The girls had silky hair, always coloured. They were grown up and their bodies were developed and they had their own purses like grown-ups do. They would be fashionably dressed in the latest tank tops and miniskirts and they would be reciprocating all the flirtatious gestures thrown at them with equal ardour; a lascivious pat here, a tickly nudge there. I wanted to grow up to reach that phase. I thought someday I would be here in such a situation too, with a new boy every two months. While none of that had happened during my college days, it was sort of happening now, but no one might have looked at us like I used to look at all those people. Neither Harsh nor I was the conventionally good-looking type. No little girl would be looking at me from afar and hoping to become like me when she was older. No matter how much we all evolve and realize that intellect and inner beauty are inimitable traits, there's no denying that outer beauty is most appealing.

Coffee with Harsh was a confusing affair. There was no firm verdict in my mind as we progressed towards the end of our date. When the bill came, I offered to pay, saying he could pay the next time—my way of checking whether there would be a next time. I'm so sly, it's awesome! Harsh took me up on my offer with little hesitation and it made for a refreshing change. The whole operation had lasted for about an hour. Poor Father must have been home for just fifteen to twenty minutes before I asked him to pick me up again.

On my way home, I analysed everything. I could tell that Father wanted to ask me several questions but hesitation was etched all over his face. I had to decide what I would tell my family before we reached home.

The positives were that Harsh was quiet, simple, straightforward and soft-spoken. On the other hand, these traits also made him boring. For every good point there was a bad one and vice versa. How the hell did people decide such matters?

There was still no verdict even as Father stationed our car into the parking spot. There was a flurry of questions as soon as I set foot in the house. It made me nervous. They sat me down full round-table-conference style and began asking question after question.

'But why are you back so soon?' mom inquired repeatedly.

'How many girlfriends has he had?'

'Are you going to meet him again?'

The worst one was, 'Did he try to kiss you?'

No points for guessing who asked that one.

At the end of the chat, I was quite upset that my meeting with Harsh hadn't lasted for hours (like how Anu described hers had when she first met Akshay). I knew it was wrong to do this but I had started drawing comparisons between Anu's story and mine from day one. It did nothing except make me feel worse about myself.

After dinner, Mother came into my room and asked me what my take on the matter was. Did I want to see Harsh again? Was there any use pursuing the matter further? Could I see my future with him? I had spent the entire evening thinking about such questions. I tried to weigh the pros against the cons but the possibility that Harsh would turn me down now after a one-on-one meeting was killing my confidence. I wanted to know what he thought about me. Did my job interest him? Did he find the roundness of my face cute? Was the mole on my nose too repulsive? Did my freshly threaded eyebrows make a difference? Was he going to say 'yes'?

I didn't want to be the only one to say 'yes'. That would make me look like a loser. I wanted to know what he would say before I gave my answer but there was no way of finding out. So bravely and reluctantly, I gave my family a green signal for a few more meetings with Harsh. Now I just had to wait and see what the verdict from the other side would be.

12

349 days before the wedding

'Wake up, drunkard!' a playful, mocking voice said on the other end as I answered the incessant ringing of my phone, still half asleep.

Drunkard? Me? I suddenly sat up in bed with a jolt. It was broad daylight. And my head was throbbing. I looked around my room to find garments strewn all over. What the hell had happened the night before?

Let's go back a little in the story.

13

350 days before the wedding

Anu's wedding mania had begun. It was the day of her *sangeet*-cum-cocktail party. Many Indian weddings include music and dance events a day or two prior to the ceremony. Some families include cocktails on such occasions and teetotallers like me who get introduced to them at such events don't know when to stop.

If Anu's lavish engagement a few months ago was anything to go by, then it was only obvious that her wedding would be a grand affair. And she would look like a queen. I haven't described her engagement yet because it was the same old story—she looked amazing (perfect hair, gorgeous outfit, make-up on point), Akshay looked incredible, the rings were beautiful, the ceremony was beautiful, I felt lonely, left out and jealous. Bleh.

It had been a few days since my coffee date with Harsh. In the interim, there had been no verdict from his family. My father had rung up senior Mr Tripathi a day after our coffee date to communicate my response. However, before he could do so, he was told that they would get back to him in a few days since 'some urgent matter was being dealt with in the family'. We all knew what that meant! At least I did. It was time to bid adieu to this boy as well. But the day Anu's wedding celebrations began, I vowed not to be affected by anything boy-related for the duration of the wedding. This was not the time to cry over my most definite lifelong virginity.

So, on the night of Anu's cocktail party I made my best effort to doll up as per the norms. For the first time, I wore a lehenga—the dress code for Anu's girlfriends. I teamed it with a long blouse perfectly tailored to cover all skin on my torso. I had bought shiny new clothes for every occasion. I even wore heels!

Disha (another friend) and I got our hair done at the beauty parlour near her house. She instructed the hairdresser to make 'soft curls' on my hair. 'Wow!' she exclaimed when I was ready. But when I saw myself, it looked as if I had been given an electric shock. Why would I pay someone to look like this? I expressed my displeasure to Disha without making it look like a complaint but she assured me that it was amazing and that I was just not used to it. She then put 'professional' make-up on me at her house. Disha was a make-up artist for some not-so-well-known celebrities but she knew her job well. She spoke a little gibberish while trying to explain concepts like 'baking', 'strobing' and 'cooking' in make-up, whatever they meant.

With every layer that she added on my face, I grew more conscious of it. 'Don't worry, I'm doing it as per the occasion,' she said on seeing my sceptical expression. When she was done, I genuinely wondered if she had dressed me up for Halloween! I felt obliged to praise her though I didn't feel confident pulling the look off at all. It was going to be one long uncomfortable night.

To add to my misery, Disha's boyfriend Arpit, who was also invited to the wedding, was picking us up to take us to the party, making me feel like a clingy third wheel.

At the venue, we were early. We went on stage and rehearsed the dance that we were to perform. Sangeet performances are the average person's opportunity to feel like a superstar, to have one's moment in the spotlight, to show one's moves, to show the world that we could all have become Shah Rukh Khans and Katrina Kaifs had we wanted to. I was nervous. I didn't mind being in some corner of one brief performance for the sake of feeling involved and important in my best friend's wedding but Anu was making me take centre stage for three dance performances in a row. That left too much room for mistakes.

Once the venue started filling up, the bride and groom made their grand entry, hand-in-hand. Anu looked ethereal in a purple jacket lehenga, which was all the rage back then and I grew a little green with envy. Akshay looked even better than her, in a fitted sherwani (obviously it was purple too) that hugged his body deliciously and I grew a little red with lust. Not an ounce of make-up on him and yet so good-looking. Boys don't get enough credit for looking effortlessly good.

Everyone hummed appreciative sounds as if they were eating juicy pieces of chicken when the couple slowly, enticingly, walked through the crowd. The two made a few stops to greet some elders and eventually made their way to the throne-like seat designed especially for them to sit on and view the performances from.

The run-up to my performance was nerve-racking. I don't even know why I had butterflies in my stomach. The bar had opened a while ago and Disha and gang started drinking. Everyone insisted that I have a drink, despite my refusal more than once. I wasn't for or against drinking. It was just unfamiliar territory. In college, I had tried a few neat shots of vodka that had made me regret my existence the next morning.

Eventually, on insistence of Disha's boyfriend, who seemed like a genuinely nice man, I agreed for ONE glass of wine. By the time I had to go up on stage for my performance I had gulped down three. And by the end of the night, one glass had turned into one bottle. No wonder I didn't remember what happened next. Damn peer pressure!

14

349 days before the wedding

'Wake up, drunkard!' a playful, mocking voice said on the other end as I answered the incessant ringing of my phone, still half asleep.

Drunkard? Me? I suddenly sat up in bed with a jolt. It was broad daylight. And my head was throbbing. I looked around my room to find garments strewn all over. What the hell had happened the night before?

'Hello? Are you there?' Disha's voice blared into my ears again.

'Yes, yes, hello. Sorry.'

'Just wanted to check if you were still alive.'

I didn't understand.

'Why, what happened?'

'You don't remember?' she said and laughed. What was this now? 'I'm not surprised. Well, check your phone later. Anyway, please hurry up and reach Anu's house as soon as possible. Aunty needs a lot of help. And Anu is panicking. Actually, come to the hotel directly.'

'Okay,' I managed to say, still confused. I felt uneasy. Something wasn't right. I had probably overdone the drinking, but there was no time to ponder over it. It was the day of Anu's wedding. I had to rush.

Quickly, I tried to tidy the room. By that I mean I bunched up the things that were scattered, into one neat pile of mess to be tackled with later. A quick shower and an unsatisfying breakfast later, I rushed out of the house. All the haste made my head throb even harder but there wasn't a moment to stop. The family didn't suspect anything thanks to my reputation of a teetotaller.

It was only during the ride to the hotel that I found a moment or two to check my phone. Nonchalantly, I opened a few chat windows and suddenly it started coming back to me in bits and pieces—drunken, hazy memories of drunken, hazy moments from the previous night. What I had done?

Sudden panic gripped me. Something terribly embarrassing had happened and I got more and more convinced of this with every passing second. Somehow, I thought of Harsh. Why? What did this have to do with him? He wasn't even there at the event. But I remembered him, something of him. At this point, the cab driver asked me for directions and I got a bit derailed from my immediate train of thought. I was drawing a complete blank save a few random traces of what must have happened. A man laughing uncontrollably. Was it

Disha's boyfriend? There was the performance onstage. I remember climbing unsteadily on to the stage, some part of my outfit getting stuck somewhere, under somebody's foot? Oh god! It was my foot that had got squashed under someone else's! I remembered almost victoriously and bent down to check my right foot. But there was no injury. It seemed fine. I checked the other one and there it was! A devilish bruise marred my little toe, which was by no means 'little'. The bruise didn't hurt. Hmmm.

What else had happened? At this point, the cab driver sped past an empty road and as the wind blew in my face I caught a whiff of something mildly foul. I quickly rolled up the window to bar the stench and to stop my untamed hair from blowing into my face. Oddly enough, the smell continued to invade my nostrils. It was vomit! And it was coming from my hair. What a gross situation to be in! I examined my hair but it seemed clean, save for a few sticky strands. It was now getting more and more important to know what had happened and I had to uncover the mystery before facing the same set of people again.

Quickly, nervously, I went into the photo gallery of my phone for any clues to trace the events of the previous night and my heart jumped at what I saw. There were tonnes of photographs taken at the party. In the first one, I seemed to be cheering a crowd of people onstage with my fingers in my mouth as if I were about to whistle. I CANNOT whistle so this is ridiculous! In the next one, I was doing a weird dance move. The angle was so pathetic that I would have liked to have a word or two with the photographer. If there were ever a need to make myself look bigger than I am then, this is the person I would go to. In the next picture, I was dancing with a man I had NEVER seen before in my life. Did I embarrass Anu and her family?

I quickly flipped through the rest of the images. Some didn't feature me but that wasn't a great consolation. Then I went through my call logs and there they were! Three calls to Harsh. Yes, I had drunk-dialled him. This was bad. The details showed an outgoing call to him, a return call from him and an outgoing call to him again. This was really bad. I shuddered to imagine what might have transpired between us. Why did I call him? How could I have no clear memory of the conversation? I thought of calling Disha so she could fill me in on the horrors I had committed at Anu's cocktail party, but I had already reached the hotel by then and there was not a minute to waste.

Unsure of how I would be received by the people who might have witnessed my drunkenness, I warily walked into the lobby, trying my best to avoid anyone's gaze. However, I was met with smiles and glares from at least three people, whom I did not recognize. I would figure it all out later, now it was time to console Anu since she had woken up to a mighty pimple on her right cheek.

* * *

Once I reached the bride's suite, everything happened in fast-forward mode. It was manic. Anu's mom was fretting over something that was to be arranged by them but had been forgotten. Anu was fretting over the ridiculous zit that had magically erupted on her face that morning. Anu's father was fretting that everyone around him was fretting.

While Anu took a shower and got ready, I ran around for some last-minute errands. At one point, I didn't even know where I was headed and for what. From helping Anu eat with all the face painting going on, to helping her use the washroom once she was in her rigid bridal garment, I did everything. And I couldn't stop imagining my wedding day throughout the process. Why did girls stress so much over this so-called most important day of their lives? Since the moment I had entered, I had not seen happiness on Anu's face even once. There was just stress. Stress about pimples, about garments not fitting well, about having magically woken up with a paunch (which was not true. If what Anu had was a paunch then what I had was an overdue baby!). Not only Anu, everyone around her also seemed to be in a frenzy.

Time flew that day. Before I even realized it, I was already escorting Anu into the hall along with the rest of the girls. With a lot of brouhaha and *shorsharaba*, the groom made his grand entry in a carriage. I can't even begun to say how handsome he looked. Anu was one lucky girl and Akshay one lucky guy! Theirs was truly a fairy-tale arrangement.

Once the pandit started reciting mantras, I got hold of Disha and asked her to fill me in on the night before.

'You seriously don't remember anything?'

'Does it look like I'm joking?'

'How much did you drink, girl?'

'Disha, don't lecture, just tell me!'

'You had a crazy time, that's all.'

'That's all?'

'Okay, that would be putting it too mildly. Basically, you stole the show during the performances. I don't know what got into you. You dragged Akshay into our performance at the end, totally impromptu and . . .'

'What!'

'How can you not remember?'

'You know what! Maybe I do. Is that when someone stamped my foot?'

'Yes,' Disha said sheepishly. It could not have been her. I could swear it seemed like a much heavier person.

'Arpit felt so bad about it, he drove me mad asking me to ensure if you were okay.' Arpit was her boyfriend, in case you've forgotten.

'You called him Armpit!'

'What? Oh god. What else happened?'

'I don't know, I was pretty drunk myself. You did vanish for a while. I remember looking for you. I found you in the girls' washroom on the phone but you swore you weren't talking to anyone.'

That explained it! That's when I must have dialled Harsh. Now there was no other way to find out what had happened, except calling Harsh, but I didn't have the nerve to do so. Disha looked like she was going to probe further but I changed the topic before she could.

'And then we went home?'

'Are you kidding? That's when the party started! We had two more rounds of tequila shots and hit the dance floor. Seriously, in all these years of knowing you, I'd never taken you for a dancer, but you owned it. You and that uncle brought the house down!'

'Uncle? Did you just say "Uncle"?'

Disha laughed hard though I was not amused.

'Yes! Akshay's mother's cousin or someone. He's the over-enthu type, knows all the lyrics and the choreography of every Bollywood song ever made. And you matched him step for step.'

'What are you saying?'

'I can't believe you don't remember.'

'I can't believe you're talking about me. Okay, point out the uncle to me without being obvious.'

'I don't think he's come today. Maybe his wife has grounded him,' she laughed again. 'She's the one in the green saree. Second row.'

'Oh my god, that's his wife! No wonder she's been giving me dirty looks all day. I thought I was imagining it.'

'No wonder, indeed!'

* * *

Watching Anu get married Akshay was an emotional experience for me. When would I see this day? When would I find a man who would look at me the way Akshay looked at Anu? What if I never found someone like that? Would any man look beyond the reality of my body and fall in love with my nature, my mind? Was it really possible in this day of Photoshop and filters?

Once the wedding rituals were over, Anu was a lot more relaxed. Finally, I saw a hint of happiness on her face. Throughout the ceremony, Akshay could be seen whispering sweet nothings into her ear and on cue she would blush or laugh. At one point, she got a little emotional and he magically got her to smile again. The guests were having orgasms just watching them.

Towards the end of the ceremony, I had tears in my eyes. Onlookers thought they were tears of happiness for my friend, but the truth was I was sad for myself. In everything we do, we inevitably end up thinking about ourselves.

After the rituals got over, it was time for the wedding reception. Anu quickly slipped from the crowd that was eager to meet her, to change into another dress. Since the celebrations had begun, this was the first time I had a few private moments with my friend. We sat in the bride's suite as she removed her ornaments (only to put on new ones). Suddenly, she approached me and asked me to find Akshay's name on her henna-stained hands.

The mehendi ceremony, held prior to the wedding, is an ancient tradition of applying henna on the bride's hands and writing the groom's name somewhere in the intricate pattern. It's quite a naughty tradition because apparently until the groom finds his name, he can't bed his wife on the wedding night. So, to make matters interesting, his name is written as illegibly as possible.

This was the only time in the whole day, when Anu seemed excited about something. It was not hard to spot Akshay's name in the gaps between her fingers and I told her the same. She laughed.

'It's good that it won't take long to find it. I don't intend to waste too much time,' she said and winked, but I couldn't bring myself to reciprocate genuinely.

Anu and Akshay had that sexual dimension, that catalyst of attraction between them. It was so obvious, so clear. Anu was confident about her wedding night. She was looking forward to it. I could not even imagine how it would be to be naked and in bed with a man.

Even if by some miracle I could find a man I liked who by some miracle also liked me in return, would I be able to connect with him that way? How would I muster the courage to bare it all in front of him, not just my (large) body, but my sense of love and loving? Just thinking about it nauseated me. I'd not even been remotely intimate with a man. How would it be? How would I manage? What if I couldn't? What if he couldn't? Anu's wedding had managed to open yet another Pandora's box in my life.

15

347 days before the wedding

It was the day after Anu's wedding. I woke up in a bad mood, sulking that my best friend, a girl I'd known for the longest time, was now someone's wife. And even though this didn't actually make her superior to me in any way, it bothered me. She had added another identity to herself. She had progressed to the next stage of life and I felt like I was falling behind. I could not see it happening for me, not in the near future. I did harbour a little bit of guilt for sulking over someone else's happiness but I couldn't stop feeling like that. Fat girls make themselves susceptible to constant comparison. It starts with a comparison of the body but soon snakes its way to every other aspect of life. And it all boils down to one problem, one quality, one so-called imperfection—being fat. You tend to start blaming it for everything. And I knew all this. I knew I was being too hard on myself. I knew that there was enough about myself that I could appreciate but I just wasn't brave enough.

I thought of how Anu's first marital night might have been and it made me feel gross and jealous at the same time. I didn't want to picture it. I didn't desire to be with a man so intimately, it terrified me, but I wanted it too. It was not an easy space to be in, but I had other things to worry about—like figuring out what the hell I had said to a prospective husband over a drunken phone call.

In my heart of hearts, I knew that I had spoilt whatever *slim* chance there had been of things working out between Harsh and me. There was no hope of a mature conversation between us over that call. My best guess and only logical conclusion was that it was a stupid, inappropriate call made at an inappropriate time in a very inappropriate state. Other than being fat, I was now probably also the badly behaved, uncultured and shameless girl. The Tripathis would never accept me.

Apart from figuring out what had happened, I also had to prepare a way to explain my antics to my family if it came to that. Suppose Harsh had spewed out everything to his parents? They would now call mine not only to reject the proposal but also give them a good talking to? How embarrassing would that be for my father to endure! He would be absolutely ashamed. Mother would reprimand me. Grandma might be proud though.

I reluctantly got out of bed hoping everyone would be done with breakfast so I wouldn't have to face them, but when I peeped out of the door, I saw them waiting in the usual round-table-conference-style around the dining table. It had happened. The call had come. I could feel it in the atmosphere, the quietness of the house, the sombreness on my grandmother's face. I could recognize my family's tension the way I could read their happiness or grief.

I started pacing my room in order to think of an excuse, an explanation, a way out with my dignity intact. The only problem was that I didn't know what the problem was. I tried to take a guess. My personality would not have allowed me to be too rude no matter what my state. Or would it? I hadn't ever been that drunk before. The worst I could have done was say *harsh* things to Harsh for not accepting the proposal. But they hadn't outright rejected me either, so I could not have jeopardized the situation further no matter how drunk I was. But the mood outside my room indicated how serious the matter was.

I decided to dive into the situation and face it. The easiest way out would be to listen to the offences I was charged with, accepting that I had got drunk and out of hand, apologizing and listening to their rant. *Tomorrow everything will be okay again.* I had to face the music for now.

Trying to be as nonchalant as possible, I went out and greeted everyone. Everybody responded normally. There was no immediate lambasting and to evade it altogether, I scooted off to the kitchen on the pretext of getting myself a glass of milk.

A minute passed, then two, then three and hope rose in my heart that maybe I had misjudged the situation after all. Harsh had been kind enough to not be complaining and my drunken antics would forever remain a secret. I started to pour milk into a glass when my father called, causing my hand to shake and some milk to spill on the kitchen countertop.

Damn! So close.

'Yes, Papa, I'm just getting my breakfast.'

'Come here, we need to discuss something.' We always needed to 'discuss something' those days. It was getting tiring. Getting married is bloody tough, especially when you're *not* getting married.

My skin started prickling. Never had I thought that I would get scolded by my father for drunk-dialling a boy who could have been my husband (but would not be because I drunk-dialled him in the first place!). I paced the kitchen a little. *Why am I being so jumpy?* I asked myself. *I am a grown-up, independent woman, who just had a little more to drink than she should have and used her phone a little more than she should have. I don't deserve to be yelled at for that. I've got this.*

I gave myself the most rubbish pep talk in the history of rubbish pep talks and prepared for my doom.

'Madhu?' came Mother's voice and I knew I couldn't avoid it any longer. Well, no point crying over spilt milk, quite literally!

'Coming, coming,' I said, walking out casually. I was going to play innocent till the end.

'How was Anu's wedding?' Mother asked. Small talk before the scolding. Nice touch.

'It was very nice. You both should have come, mom, dad.'

'They didn't call,' Grandma said with a note of finality.

'Of course, they did. The invite said '& family' and Anu herself told me twice to tell you, which I did.'

'But they didn't call on the phone.'

'Oh, come on!'

'Leave matters that are beyond your understanding.'

I could sense an argument building up when Father interrupted.

'Anyway, we have something else to discuss.'

There was a rumbling in the pit of my stomach. I had not been scolded for a long time.

'The Tripathis called this morning,' Father said gravely.

'Really?' I expressed surprise. Innocent until proven guilty.

'Yes,' said Grandma, firmly.

I started to count, mentally tuning the conversation out of my head.

'We weren't expecting this.'

Ten, nine . . .

The voice became softer. Not really, I just stopped paying attention. I went back to that night. I tried to picture myself dialling Harsh. The voices of my family members reduced to a whisper but were still audible.

'Yes, we thought the matter was closed.'

Six, five . . .

I pictured myself in the washroom cubicle as Disha had described. And suddenly I remembered a moment. A moment when I saw his number flash on my phone. He had called me back for something. Even my call log suggested the same. Why had he called back?

Three, two . . .

'I can't believe they have said "Yes".'

I was thinking of that moment. Why had he called me back?

One!

'WHAT?!!' I cried out on realizing what I had heard. My attention shot back to the present.

'Don't act so surprised. We know you and Harsh have spoken about this already.'

Now that was a double whammy! It took every ounce of my willpower from yelling again. I regained my composure, trying to process everything but it was impossible to believe it. This was the second time Harsh had managed to surprise me by offering acceptance when I had expected rejection.

'They want an engagement soon and the wedding within six months.'

Was there something called a triple whammy? What the hell was happening? Was I still drunk from that night?

'I wish you had told us that you and Harsh were still in touch. We had approached a few more families because we thought that it was a closed chapter,' said Mother.

'Yes, exactly. And we would not have been as tongue-tied had we been told to expect it. Quite a little *chhupa Rustam* you are,' Grandma said in mock anger, trying hard to contain her naughty smile.

My head started to spin with confusion. Was I getting married? Was I getting married to Harsh? Was that a good thing? I didn't know what to feel. I didn't know the reason behind Harsh's sudden decision to marry me. I was certain it had to do with the phone call. But what that something was would remain a mystery for a while.

'Now we need to know what your final answer is. Do you want to marry that sissy little fellow?'

'Stop it, Ma,' my mother chided her mother.

'Are you denying that he is sissy?'

'I don't understand these fancy terms. All I know is that he is a good boy from a good family,' Mother answered.

'Good family, my foot!' came Grandma's sharp reply. She got a nasty glance from mother, enough to silence her.

'Why are you so against it?' I asked her, truly bewildered. Weren't they the ones who got me this proposal to begin with?

'Because now she likes another family better. The one we were planning to approach next weekend,' Mother said.

'Nothing like that,' Grandma protested weakly.

'Okay, enough of all this. This is a serious matter. Madhu, beta, what is your final answer? Do you want this? Should we go ahead and start planning an engagement?'

Oh! How badly had I wanted to experience this! This moment of final acceptance, this moment of celebration. My wedding! There was a rush of excitement in my body. It had nothing to do with Harsh or his family or with the (non-existent) connection between us. No. This was about me. This felt validating, like I, too, had a (love) life now. I, too, would have someone to go on dates with, to go to movies with. I, too, was good enough to be someone's daughter-in-law. I, too, was desired by a man. I was getting married! I would not die alone. I would not die a virgin. This was the best news in a long time. There was something ominous in the air that filled me with a sense of foreboding because it wasn't usual for someone to readily bring home a fat bride without even knowing her. However, in the excitement of my newfound validation I didn't dwell on the thought for long.

At that point, it was not Harsh when I really cared about. It could have been any other man and I would have been equally elated. It was his identity in my life that made it exciting—the possible boyfriend, the probable husband. It gave me a thrill, a stamp that I was in sync with the world, doing the things an average person does.

Most people aspired to stand out, but I always dreamed of *fitting in*. I wanted to blend into the crowd, live life like the girl next door. Being the odd one out can get tiring and I was done with being that—the fat girl.

16

341 days before the wedding

It was by far the most anticipated day at home. The day my family had been fervently waiting for. The day the burden of finding a groom would be lifted off their shoulders. The day my grandmother would get a new topic to discuss with her relatives. The day Father would find something new to worry about. The day Mother could happily begin complaining about the work to be done for her daughter's wedding. Parents love this sort of serious planning, don't they?

So that day, Harsh's family was visiting us to seal the deal and take matters further. Since the suspicious news of a green signal from the Tripathis, there had been no contact between Harsh and me. How boring, right? The last interaction we had had was the one I had no memory of. It was a confusing situation. I was more curious than ever about his sudden decision to marry me but I didn't have the nerve to contact him. Not again.

Harsh and his parents, (minus the sister—yay!) reached our place at 9 p.m. sharp.

Mother had paid extra attention to setting up the house. Grandma had paid extra attention to the setting of her hair and Father was finding it difficult to pay attention to anything at all. He seemed more nervous than me.

For the first fifteen minutes after their arrival, I was holed up in my bedroom dressed in a bright blue saree that I hadn't been able to talk myself out of wearing. Because the door was shut, I couldn't clearly hear what was going on outside, just a laugh or a sound every few minutes that confirmed the presence of several people on the other side.

When I heard my mother's knock summoning me, a shiver ran down my spine. How would I face Harsh? I couldn't stop myself from taking one last look in the mirror, an otherwise rarely used object in my room. My reflection deflated my spirits. I wish something could deflate my body as easily. I didn't at all look like a bride-to-be. In fact, in the starched saree, with the outdated (though beautiful) jewellery and the 'aunty bun', I resembled a woman who must have married and mothered at least two children several years ago. I felt angry, frustrated and panicky. I was fat, yes, but why couldn't I still feel beautiful?

I conveyed my displeasure to my mother.

'Come on, Madhu. Put a smile on your face and let's go.'

'I'm looking horrible.'

'No, you are not,' she said firmly, not elaborating further, not pacifying me, not praising me.

I never took the praise of my family members seriously. I felt it was always out of sympathy or because they were my parents. However, at that point, even some false praise would have helped me feel better. Mother didn't humour me though.

'Madhu, you are grown up now, about to get married. This childish behaviour won't do. Hurry up. Everyone is waiting.'

I went out of the room with a slightly less sullen face.

For the first seven or eight minutes, I avoided Harsh's gaze altogether and for most of the rest of the evening, he avoided mine. I just didn't understand him. His shyness was off-putting. Maybe 'shyness' was too polite a term. Maybe he was outright cold. And I don't know if it was just my imagination, but I felt that Harsh's mother had a different tone, a different demeanour, a different air about herself that day. Was she already moving into the snooty mother-in-law zone? Was she displaying pomp because she was the groom's mother? Or was she being arrogant because they were accepting me in spite of how fat I was? I wasn't sure what the reason was, but certainly, this wasn't the same woman who had been much friendlier on our previous meeting.

Most of the dinner proceedings went by predictably. There was superfluous laughter, forced chitchat, unnecessary praising and the usual. I had been unable to eat properly all day and my appetite made a fierce comeback in the middle of the evening but obviously, I couldn't ask for dinner to be served earlier. Once the elders had had enough of beating about the bush, they got down to business. I was asked to sit beside Harsh. I nervously sank into the sofa next to him. At least two people were talking to me but I couldn't take my mind off the fact that my left thigh was touching his right. I could feel tension in his body, in his posture and it made me all the more uncomfortable. Did he even want this? Had I blackmailed him into this? Why was he being so uptight?

Father handed over a coconut along with an envelope containing one thousand rupees in cash to Harsh. A basket of fruits was also given to his family as a token of confirmation. Harsh's mother reciprocated the gesture by handing over another fancy basket to us. 'There are dry fruits in this. Five kilos in total,' she said with a snobbish smile.

Throughout the evening, Harsh remained more reserved than usual. He didn't make much eye contact with me and spoke only when spoken to. The only words he had said directly to me were, 'Yes,' when I offered him another helping of rice and 'No, thank you,' when I had offered him another helping of dessert.

I know I couldn't expect him to be romantic with me in the midst of everything, but his lukewarm behaviour frustrated me further. All this suddenly felt unreal.

Sometime later, both fathers went into a corner to discuss serious matters. I learnt later that the groom's side had asked for an engagement ceremony to be held within the next fortnight in order to announce the news to near and dear ones. They wanted it to be a small affair. My father, on the contrary, had not wanted an engagement at all, for it meant added expenditure, but he could not refuse, not when they were accepting his daughter into their household.

Father's sense of indebtedness towards the groom's side had been established right from the beginning. In general, too, we see the groom's side dictating terms but in my case, it was more so because, well, you know why.

Right after they left that night, Grandma and Mother started a fierce discussion on clothes and jewellery as if they were born to do this. Not even five minutes later, the doorbell rang again. I was in my bedroom.

'Madhu,' my mother said with a naughty smile. 'Harsh has come. Go.'

My heart started to race. I had just started to undo my saree. Hastily, I draped it back on. He'd come back to meet me. To talk to me. To talk to me alone! To say something that would make me smile, to make all this feel right. For the first time all day I felt how a bride-to-be should be—excited, shy and giddy.

'Hi,' I said, standing at the entrance of my house. Harsh was still outside. My family had steered clear, though I could sense Grandma's eyes peeping from behind some door or another.

'Come, come in. Why are you standing at the door?' I said sweetly, wondering what we would do now, what we would say, where his family had gone and how he would go back.

'Actually, I've forgotten my car keys,' Harsh said simply.

'Oh!' Why hadn't he just taken the keys from my mother then?

Naturally, I felt silly. This boy was almost allergic to romance. Would it be like this, like we were doing a business deal all along? This was not the bargain I had wanted to settle for. All of my adult life I had been deprived of experiencing love and lust. I deserved to be chased, to be flirted with, to be romanced. I had thought that the Love Gods had finally decided to shower their blessings on me, but I was mistaken.

With obvious disappointment, I handed over the car key to Harsh and bade him goodbye.

After a reasonable amount of sulking, I decided to be 'mature' about this. I would have to be patient. There was no need for desperation. He was marrying me of his own accord. For now, I could gloat over the fact that I was GOING TO GET MARRIED.

I would be calling my friends to give them news about ME, *I* would be shopping for bridal clothes, *I* would be planning functions and events. *I* would be the bride, the centre of attention, the one for whose wedding many people would come. The hype excited me at that time because I couldn't foresee what was coming next.

17

320 days before the wedding

The obligatory engagement that Harsh's family had wanted was just a week away and matters with him were still as stagnant as before. But who had time to worry about that? There were bigger problems to tackle, like not having anything to wear. Yes! It was a week to the big day and I had nothing to wear. Can you imagine! The crisis was real. And I was panicking.

'Don't worry. Dieting is helping. God wants you to be in better shape when you find your engagement dress,' Mother said. Which shape was she talking about? Round? You might think a weeklong of morning jogs and tasteless food could make you skinny but trust me, it doesn't.

After a very healthy and highly unsatisfying meal, Mother and I left for shopping for the third time in a week. This time I was actually eager to shop. Not having anything to wear and thus running the high risk of looking stupider than I had imagined at my engagement was worrying the crap out of me.

I hated all the options in the first shop that we went to. In the second one, I agreed to try a few outfits but didn't like them on me. I had not come to terms with the fact that I would have to compromise on the look that I had always had in my head.

As a *growing* girl, I had looked at marriage as something that would happen in the distant future, almost in another lifetime. As I grew up and the distant future turned into the immediate future, I still didn't consider marriage as something that was about to happen.

I'd always look at pictures of brides, of bridal models in magazines and try to picture myself as one. 'I'll do this to my hair,' I would tell myself on seeing a hairdo I liked. 'I would never want to look like that,' I would think on seeing an OTT bride. 'I'll lose the weight.' 'I'll let my bangs grow out.' 'I'll eat well.' 'I'll sleep more.' 'I'll go for a skin treatment.' Oh, the promises were endless and now suddenly that phase had arrived. The imaginary wedding was actually happening and the weight was still there, the pimples refused to budge, the bangs weren't growing fast enough. Reality is more real than perfectly white teeth and a tummy without tyres. The magical phase that a girl dreams of since her childhood is just a picture painted by glossy magazines. Not everyone can look as beautiful as a 'photoshopped' celebrity. Of course, I hadn't the maturity to understand any of this. I just wanted to be a beautiful bride, heck,

I wanted to be the most beautiful bride. But could a fat bride be that?

As we entered the fourth shop, Mother thought I was being too fussy and stubborn. I totally was. Maybe I was just hungry. Eventually we came home, tired and without an outfit.

Anu called that evening. She was very happy and excited for me, as were my other girlfriends. On our group chats, the constant discussions now revolved around MY engagement. It gave me a thrill of importance, of *fitting in*. Almost all my girlfriends already had something or the other to wear. Anu, especially, had a wardrobe full of gorgeous outfits thanks to her designer trousseau.

'Why are you sounding so low?' she asked on the phone.

'Nothing, ya. Forget it.'

'Why is our bride-to-be not excited? It's only a week to your big day.'

'Still don't have an outfit,' I admitted.

'What! Come, let's go shopping. Meet me at the chowk in thirty minutes?' Anu had come to her parents' house for a week.

'No, no.'

'What no! I know the best places for wedding outfits. Just come.'

'But . . .'

'No "but". I'll convince your mom if you want.'

'No, that's okay. See you.'

I told Mother I wanted to go shopping with Anu. She wasn't too pleased.

'Again today? We'll go tomorrow.'

'No. I'm going with her. She knows the best places anyway. You don't know anything,' I snapped.

I don't exactly remember what I was so upset about. I think it all boiled down to being unhappy with how I looked and would look on all the occasions ahead of me. When you're unhappy with yourself, you end up offloading your frustration on people who you know will put up with it. It's the ugly truth.

Anu took me to shops I had not even heard about before. She had recently returned from her extravagant honeymoon in some exotic place called Saint Lucia. I had actually Googled where it was when she told me. Naturally, she had a lot to tell me about it. I feigned enthusiasm but despised myself for not being genuinely happy for her.

A big problem while shopping with Anu was the budget. She took me to fancy shops where everything was obscenely expensive. You'd think they made garments with real diamonds! Eventually, I think she understood that I wanted something in a range much lower than she'd reckoned.

It wasn't as if we were poor or anything. My parents could afford one or two lavish outfits for me, but they would rather spend money on valuable items like gold and silver, which were more of an 'investment', than clothes and shoes.

At the third shop with Anu, I was shown a few outfits that were not as expensive as the others. Being a working woman, I could splurge a little on myself. I could chip in where the amount exceeded my mother's budget.

However, once the price stopped being the problem, it was the style. I wasn't very much in sync with the latest trends those days. When nothing fits you, you tend not to follow fashion trends.

Anu's reaction to every outfit I tried was like my mother's would have been—everything made me look 'gorgeous' apparently. I know she was just trying to be nice but at that point I felt like a child who has to be praised falsely so that she doesn't feel bad about the truth.

It was obvious that the lehenga choli style was not working out for me. I had to let go of some stunning designs and some reasonably priced outfits because they made me look like a huge ball of fabric. Anu realized I wanted something that would not expose my arms, stomach and back, in fact anything other than my face.

Next, we tried 'Indian gowns', whatever the hell that meant! Some of the garments were beautiful, no doubt, but they made me look amazingly pregnant. I'm sure the salespersons thought I'd come to shop for my baby shower.

We got down to inspecting traditional Indian garments that had offered more cover-up than the others. Anu got hooked on to one with an asymmetrical design, the hem of which was lopsided, sloping from above my left knee and then going down to my right ankle. The long top had fringed layers and there were pants underneath. It was a confusing pattern but Anu assured me the style was all the rage. Even the combination was a bit jarring—shades of purple merging with pink. I was not convinced but my fashionista friend was hung up on it.

'If you're not buying it, I'm buying it for you. So either way it's yours.'

Eventually I bought it. I don't know why I was in such a rush. Maybe I just wanted to please Anu, show her that I understood fashion, let her know that she had been of help to me.

When I reached home, I knew Mother would ask me to show her what I had shopped and I didn't want to, probably because I knew she wouldn't like it, because I knew I didn't like it either. I was angry with the whole world—angry with the shops for not having better clothes for plus size girls, angry with Harsh for being the least romantic man I had ever met (not that I had met many romantic men), angry with my mother for letting me get this fat, angry with myself for getting this fat. Just angry. And hungry.

18

313 days before the wedding

It was the day of my engagement. But wait. Let's back up a little. Ever since 'the night of the mysterious phone call', Harsh and I had been having a confusing equation between us. At least I was thoroughly confused. The reluctance of his family to give us an answer at the beginning, his sudden agreement to get married after 'the night of the mysterious phone call', his indifference during the 'official' dinner at my house and his lack of initiative thereafter were making me too damn wary of him. Impotency was my topmost suspicion this time. I had ruled out homosexuality, remember? Next on the list was a hidden first marriage. The possibilities were endless.

It's not as if we didn't communicate at all. Harsh was majorly into 'forwards'. He was the type of person who would send positive messages to people in the morning. Every two days, I would wake up to a *'Good morning'*

99

message with a preachy quote that he must be sending to all the contacts on his phone. Who does that? Especially with their wife-to-be. Sigh! I would reply to his pointless message with something even more pointless like, '*Wow, what a beautiful thought*' and that's how our lacklustre conversations would often begin. Harsh was very proper, if that's the word I'm looking for. If I asked what he was doing, he would give me a description of what he was actually doing, no matter how technical or boring it was. On the plus side, I now know what a motherboard is!

Harsh wasn't as curious about my whereabouts as I was about his. There was no flirting whatsoever. This one time, I made the mistake of fishing for a compliment. '*My new haircut is looking so bad*', I texted him, hoping that not only would he say something nice but also make a plan to meet me to see the haircut. '*Do not worry, I'm sure it will grow out soon.*' he replied. He was just so absurd. He would type complete sentences, use punctuation marks, sound angry because he never used smileys. I know this doesn't sound like something to complain about, but I wasn't used to this type of conversation. He couldn't even be casual, leave alone naughty. I had reckoned a groom-to-be would be nothing but enthusiastic towards his counterpart. This was not the type of courtship I had hoped to have. But maybe this was all fat girls could get.

Now to come back to my wardrobe woes. After my shopping stint with Anu, there was another one with Mother. She hadn't given any conclusive reaction on seeing the outfit I had bought with Anu and was hell-bent on taking me shopping again. I tagged along with her from shop to shop and rejected all the options she gave me. I was directing all my anger about not looking like the perfect bride towards my mother. I sort of held her accountable for my state. I knew it wasn't right, but it always helps to share the blame.

She was insistent that I wear either a saree or a lehenga for the occasion. Considering my previous outing in a saree, I was dead against it. I had no intention of looking like Harsh's mother rather than his fiancée at our engagement. So, the saree idea was out. And the other option made me just as unhappy. In sheer defiance and stupidity, I declared that I would wear the outfit I had bought with Anu and no one could change my mind.

We had quite a heated argument over this but eventually Mother gave up. I was able to dominate in such matters since my grandmother, the undisputed decision-maker of the house, was not at home. She had gone to stay at her sister's place, our ancestral home in Old Delhi, for a few days. Some of her jewellery, which I would inherit, was kept there and on her return before my engagement, she would get it with her.

When the day finally arrived, I was more nervous than excited. Actually, I wasn't excited at all. Which girl would be if she weighed more than her groom on the day of their betrothal? And that too a groom who didn't possess the ability to have a single romantic conversation!

Anu had come down from her new house to her maternal home the previous day in order to be with me from the morning. The venue of the engagement was a nearby banquet hall that could accommodate about seventy to eighty people. Most of the guests were from Harsh's side. Most of my relatives would come directly for the wedding.

We arrived at the venue by 9 a.m. The ceremony was scheduled to take place between 11 a.m. and noon. A changing room had been provided for me to get ready in. It smelled of the toilet next to it. I had hired Anu's bridal make-up artist (who was costing me an arm and a leg), hoping for the same result that he had brought out on Anu's face. Mother, Father and Grandma had a lot of other matters to panic over, so Anu supervised matters in the changing room.

We hadn't decided on 'the look' beforehand so a lot of time was wasted in trial and error. Eventually, I told the make-up artist to replicate what he had done on Anu's face on the night of her cocktail party, without realizing that hers had been an evening affair. He told me to go for a lighter, simpler look but I insisted on going all the way hoping to look as pretty as Anu had, neck upwards at least. Obviously, he obliged and turned me into a witch at ten in the morning. Okay, maybe I'm being a bit harsh. Poor fellow did his best to replicate the look on Anu with the help of pictures from that night. Smokey eyes, dark lips, etc. At any other time and on any other person, it may have looked stunning but it didn't suit me or the occasion. I should have gone with something light, dewy, fresh for the morning as had been suggested but if we all had our common sense in place at all times then how would disasters happen?

That wasn't the last of my bad decisions. I don't know what was wrong with all of us that we decided to have my hair crimped. Yes! CRIMPED it! Who does that? I'm not sure how we got to the conclusion of crimping it but catastrophes have their own ways of occurring. When I was done, we sent for my mother and when she saw me, we all got the reality check we needed.

'Is this how you plan to get engaged?' she asked, not masking her disapproval in front of the others.

'Uh, hello, Ma'am. Do you want us to change anything?' the make-up artist offered politely.

'How about everything?'

Deathly silence followed.

'Look, we don't have time for this. If you ask me, my daughter looks nicer on a regular day to work but I guess I am too old-fashioned.'

'Just send her out in the next five minutes,' she looked towards Anu and said. Then she turned and left, without as much as a second look.

I realized she was absolutely right. The panic button had been pressed and my waterworks began. There was no time for anyone to pacify me and everyone starting undoing/redoing things on me. The lipstick was subdued, the dark eye make-up was lightened, the hair was tied into a neat bun. We did as much damage control as possible before it was time for me to be paraded in front of the guests.

I regained my composure as best as I could and went near the stage. Harsh was already there and he smiled at me as lovingly as a brother would smile at his sister.

What an idiot! There was no complimenting on his part, no blushing on mine. We stood on the stage like two puppets ready to be thrown into the sea of matrimony for the society and it's norms.

We had to greet a lot of people before the exchange of rings. First on the list was Harsh's maternal grandmother, who had come down from a remote city in Haryana. I greeted her with folded hands and said 'Namaste'. It didn't strike me that I was expected to touch her feet until my mother actually nudged me to bow. The grandmother gave me her blessings and was then escorted to the 'elders' section' (front row seating), which every wedding has right?

After her, I 'greeted' several more pairs of feet. If only this had happened a week ago, I would have had six-pack abs on my engagement day.

Thirty minutes into the greetings, the pandit summoned Harsh and me for the ring ceremony. My parents had selected a gold band for Harsh with a diamond in the middle. I hadn't been involved in the ring selection process on either side.

We were the centre of everyone's attention and our respective mothers produced the rings before us. I immediately took Harsh's ring from my mother and proceeded to slip it on to his finger. The process was clumsy, Harsh's hand limp and shaky. I remembered Anu's engagement. There was so much hooting, shrieking and filmy drama. Akshay had gone down on one knee and asked for Anu's hand.

Before I knew it, the ring was on Harsh's finger. It fitted well. Mother had done a good job. That's when panic gripped me again. I saw my ring in Harsh's mother's hand and a nasty thought occurred to me. 'It won't fit', fat Madhu's voice rang in my head. I hated her. Fat Madhu had always overshadowed Madhu. She followed me to my favourite shops in malls; she discouraged me from buying clothes I hoped to fit into. When I got clothes as presents for my birthday, she would warn me that they wouldn't fit; when I tried to convince myself I would lose weight, she would tell me it wouldn't happen. And now, she had the fat cheek to tell me that the ring wouldn't fit! I ignored her and prayed to the Skinny Gods to bestow some luck on me just for this moment. The ring had to fit or I would throw one.

A plain and delicate band of gold, it didn't boast of money, but it was beautiful all the same and it didn't look like my size. I was sure of it. I knew they would have checked my ring size with my mother but there was always scope for mistakes in such matters. Those few seconds between the exchange of both rings were sheer misery for me. How embarrassing would it be if it didn't fit in front of an audience? What would I do? How would I cover up the blunder?

Harsh took the ring in his hand after a gap long enough for me to chant the names of at least nine gods. I couldn't bring myself to offer my pudgy hand. Everyone thought I was being coy but really, I was just nervous. My palms were sweating, making my fingers swell even more. There couldn't have been a worse time for this to happen.

Mother smilingly lifted my hand and brought it to Harsh's. He began to slide the ring on my finger as my tears began to fall. It must have looked like I was getting emotional but I was crying out of relief because, though with a little difficulty, the ring fit me perfectly. Thank heavens! Fat Madhu could go take a hike! She'd lose some weight in the bargain. As for Madhu, she was now officially engaged and soon to be married.

19

295 days before the wedding

A few days had passed since my engagement. I will always regret not enjoying a single moment of my big day. But a bigger one awaited me . . .

I was back from my lectures by dinner time. College and exams had been going well for me so far, in spite of also having to manage work and the pressure of getting married.

'Oh, Madam has come,' said my grandmother, making it sound like a taunt. I knew something was up.

'Hi, Nani.'

'Your MOTHER-IN-LAW had called,' she said, stressing on the term more than necessary. Every time I realized I almost had a mother-in-law, it made me sick. Literally.

'Okay, good!' I said indifferently, trying to find a way to pacify Grandma without knowing the reason for her edginess.

'Madam has demanded that you accompany her family to a wedding. Didn't even ask if it would be okay with us. We don't send our unmarried girls like this.'

I stood quietly absorbing the news. I had no idea about this wedding, or that I would be expected to go too.

'Oh stop it, Ma,' my mother intervened. 'Stop being such a drama queen. Nita *behenji* explained perfectly well. Agreed that she didn't ask if it was okay. She said she would want to take Madhu with them. What is wrong in that? She is their daughter-in-law.'

'Not yet.'

'By all means.'

'Don't act like you know more than me about such matters, Rima.'

'Ma, enough.'

'I don't want to go,' I blurted out and suddenly everybody's focus shifted on me.

'Why not?' both women asked with concern.

'I . . . it will be so weird. I won't know anyone. I don't even have good clothes. And . . .'

'Don't be childish, Madhu. If you know them all from now on you'll already be familiar with them before your marriage. It will only help.'

I stood thinking about it. Yuck! This was *yuck*.

'Aren't you all invited too?'

'She asked us to come,' Mother said matter-of-factly.

'But they didn't send a card,' Grandma declared. And obviously my family couldn't just show up without an invitation card. Wedding politics is not a joke.

'It's just a matter of two days.'

'And besides, we don't seem to have much of a choice. Harsh's mother has expressed her desire to take you. It was nice of her. We can't say no.'

'Then that ends the discussion, I guess,' I said and went to my room to talk to Harsh.

Fifteen minutes later we were on the phone. It must have been our sixth or seventh conversation over the phone. Ever.

'So will you come?' he asked.

'I'm not sure.' I really wasn't. I would be totally out of place and at the centre of everyone's attention. The thought of being scrutinized by Harsh's extended family, of being judged for my clothes and looks, was scary. Everything I did, said and ate would be observed. There was too much scope for trouble.

And my family wouldn't even be there for moral support. I'd definitely much rather stay peacefully at home.

'Okay,' Harsh said. That's it. No convincing, no reasoning, no asking me to try to make it. It put me off completely. Why was I even doing this? Why was I marrying a man who was so wooden? A man who hadn't the courage to romance a girl he had himself agreed to marry.

I sat sulking in bed. I had not wanted to go for this event from the minute I'd heard about it but when Harsh didn't insist, I suddenly wanted to go. Or rather, I wanted to be convinced to go for it. What is it about reverse psychology? It beats me completely.

Thoroughly unsatisfied with the state of my love life, I decided to brood over the matter later and tried to sleep.

Sometime in the middle of the night, the beep of my phone woke me up. My eyes flew open when I saw it was a message from Harsh.

'*It would be nice if you could come,*' read his message. I rubbed my eyes and read again. My inexpressive, boring fiancé had made a genuine, although unusual, effort to convince me. And just like that I was baffled again. Harsh always did this. It was like walking back three steps only to take a step ahead. His behaviour was mystifying, to say the least. I checked the time. It was a little after 3 a.m. in one line. What a weirdo he was! *It would be nice if you could come.* What were we? Characters of some classic English novel?

Nonetheless, I could not bring myself to overlook his effort. It's not as if I would have been able to get out of the plan if he hadn't texted. I would have gone anyway. To Mother and Grandma, it wouldn't matter that Harsh hadn't tried to convince me. They would think I was being stupid and childish. For them, romance is stupid and childish. What does romance have to do with more important things like marriage and children? Nothing.

Too sleepy to care about any of this, I texted Harsh, 'I will come'. If anyone read the exchange between Harsh and me, they'd agree we were doing it wrong. Two people could not have been more platonic. Whatever happened to sweet nothings? I just had nothing.

20

282 days before the wedding

It was a laboriously long journey to Harsh's mother's maiden home in Fatehabad. We started on the journey in the wee hours of the morning and covered 250-odd kilometres over a five-hour-long drive in Harsh's sedan, which although was meant for five, couldn't accommodate his mother, sister and me comfortably in the back seat.

'This will be one of our last long trips in this car,' his sister said excitedly. 'Papa is buying a new car. A red one, right?'

This was news to me. I hoped the new car would be slightly bigger. The four Tripathis animatedly discussed the new member coming into their family (not me). It was being bought on the occasion of the wedding. Harsh was actually childlike while discussing the colour, features and interior of the car. He was a different man in those three minutes. Outspoken, opinionated and truly interested. Why couldn't he be like this in matters of the heart?

I remained quiet as much as possible during the journey. There was less chance of getting into trouble that way. We reached Harsh's maternal family home by lunch time. It was a palatial property that hadn't been maintained well. Paint was peeling off the walls, the house looked dilapidated. The grass in the garden was high and uncut.

Much as I was looking forward to the break from work and college, I was equally dreading the next two days. Harsh's first cousin was getting married to a girl from the same city. I had heard great things about her soft-spoken nature and beauty throughout the drive to the bungalow. Harsh's mother had been profusely praising her. Every time she said something about her figure and beauty, it felt like a taunt directed towards me, even if it weren't so. The trip would be agonizing.

Harsh's mother introduced me to her family as hurriedly as it was possible to introduce someone you didn't really want to. We had a quick lunch and then the women got down to business, wrapping last-minute gifts. Some woman, whose relationship to Harsh I could not comprehend, was kind enough to involve me in the little chores that didn't seem to end. I was glad to be busy as it meant less attention directed towards me.

I was itching to see the 'other' bride. My counterpart of sorts, the girl I'd forever be compared to in Harsh's family. It was only natural. Even if we were both loved equally, our differences would be duly noted.

Everything seemed to be in favour of this girl. She would be married before me and would already be acquainted with the family by the time I became Harsh's wife. She was a year younger than me (I don't know why I thought this was an advantage). She was conventionally good-looking and borderline skinny, thanks to yoga (Can you believe my luck?). And above all, she was a doctor. I had seen her photographs. A young, thin, beautiful doctor. How do you top that? The more I thought about her, while wrapping the gifts, the more I felt hopeless. I willed myself to stay confident and calm, even though it was only pretence. It was just a matter of few days, for now.

That evening, a small mehendi function was organized for the women on the groom's side. We sat near the veranda, dressed casually, our hands bared to henna artists. The men were indoors for a late-afternoon siesta. Harsh and I had had limited interaction since the morning. We had got friendlier with each other, but I wanted more. I wanted romance. Clichéd though it was.

Harsh's grandmother started singing a few traditional folk songs that I did not recognize. Some of the women joined in and made a racket in the name of music, using spoons and steel plates. Frankly, the cacophony was annoying. I would occasionally smile and laugh without comprehending half the jokes. I felt like an outsider. One of the girls tried to pull me in for some dancing but I

couldn't do it. Gone was the star performer of Anu's
cocktail night. Gone was her newfound confidence.
Drunk Madhu was sorely missed. Sober Madhu was no
match for her.

At night, a musical event had been organized—
nothing like the big fat cocktail programme before Anu's
wedding. Some well-known folk artist had been roped in
to sing ghazals. How boring!

We reached the venue, all decked up, by 9 p.m. A
tempo had been organized to shuttle the guests back and
forth. I wore a simple Indian suit and did my hair and
make-up to the best of my abilities but I didn't feel good
enough. I never felt good enough. My extra weight had
created an irreparable dent in my self-confidence.

Musicians and artists were already onstage as we
took our seats. Shortly after we reached, the programme
began. Neither the bride nor her family was present.
The groom's family had organized the event solely for
themselves.

Thirty minutes into the night and it was clear that
the elders were enjoying themselves while the youngsters
were getting bored and restless. What a dull event!
They should have had something more appropriate for
the younger crowd. I would not let something like this
happen at my wedding.

I stole a glance at Harsh who was sitting motionless
beside me. He was engrossed in his phone, reading some
article or another, no doubt. Harsh was a news junkie.
The little that I had got to know of him, I had discovered

that he was always abreast with current affairs. One would always find him reading news updates on his mobile phone. I suddenly felt lost, vulnerable and out of place. I was among strangers, with this strange man who had no sense of how to be with a woman, leave alone a woman he was about to marry.

I pictured myself at home, comfortably sitting on the sofa in my pyjamas, bantering with my grandmother, secretly enjoying her mindless television soaps. I longed to go back even though it had only been a few hours. Was this what my life would become? Would I ever *fit in*? All my notions of a dreamy, romantic, arranged marriage were slowly collapsing, one at a time, making me rethink my decision to get married. I couldn't help but wonder whether things would have been different had I not been fat?

21

281 days before the wedding

On the day of Harsh's cousin's wedding, I woke up uncertain of where I was. It took a moment to realize that I was attending an outstation wedding and sharing a room with my dear, darling, sweet little sister-in-law-to-be. God, I despised her. Since the time we had been allotted the same room, she had not bothered to spend a single minute with me. Except sleeping at night, she had spent every waking minute in her dear mother's room. I had noticed that she had been cold towards me right from the beginning. She would just not take the initiative to talk to me, to make me feel welcome, to develop an equation with me, even though she was apparently outgoing. She was as extroverted as her brother was introverted. Good-looking, slim and tall, she was usually talkative, but for some reason didn't seem interested in bonding with me. She wasn't rude or nasty, just indifferent and aloof.

On finding the other half of the bed empty, I understood that she was up and about already. I checked the time and to my horror saw it was a little past eleven in the morning. I should have put on the alarm and woken up at a decent hour. Grandma's shrill voice was taunting me in my head. Even in my head, I couldn't silence her! I jumped out of bed and speedily took a shower and got dressed. About twenty minutes later, I reached the living room. Everyone was already there and the groom's haldi ceremony, a tradition where a thick paste of milk, flour and turmeric is applied on a bridegroom and bride was in process. Gross.

Trying to draw as little attention to myself as possible, I stealthily went and sat next to Harsh's sister. His mother noticed me despite my best effort to blend into the crowd. 'The maharani is here,' she remarked, caustically. I made light of the comment and smiled, embarrassed. Taunts are part and parcel of marriage, my mother always said. I'd better get used to them.

Everyone was preoccupied with applying haldi on the groom's hairy chest. Unfortunately, I also saw his armpits. Ugh! An unforgivable sight. Until the previous day, I had never seen this man. And now I had seen too much of him. Why was I even here?

I tried to gauge whether M-I-L-T-B was truly upset with me. But it was difficult to do so as she usually looked sullen. Luckily, she got busy for the rest of the day and her little jibe was the only flak I received.

Harsh was conspicuously absent during the ceremony and I hadn't had a moment to think about him since I woke up.

The bond that should have been developing between us was absent. He was supposed to be the reason why I was there—the link, the conduit, binding me to the people in that house and to the family. But, when both of us had failed to forge a relationship then how could he help me develop one with his family members?

I was dragging it on. For what? For the sake of carrying out the task of marriage, for the sake of society and its traditions, for the sake of crossing marriage off my list, for the sake of others . . .

After lunch, we had to get ready and leave for the wedding ceremony at a nearby banquet hall. Finally, I would get to see the bride in person.

I gobbled down lunch in order to have more time to get ready. Since my arrival here, I'd happily forgotten all about 'eating healthy'. Religiously, I had stayed off junk food and carbohydrates for an entire week in order to look slimmer at this wedding. Even my clothes had been taken in an inch or two because I was confident of being in better shape after the week-long 'health' spree.

To my horror, everything seemed tighter when I started getting into my clothes. How could it be? I had just let myself go for a day. How could ONE day ruin the efforts and restraint of SEVEN? Maybe the tailor had got the measurements wrong and had tightened it way too much. The blouse of my saree would surely give me a cleavage at the back. Was it possible to sue the tailor?

I started losing my patience and confidence. I was cranky, irritated and homesick. I needed my mother. I needed my home. I needed some familiarity or sense of belonging. This was all so strange and frightening. Despite the paucity of time, I took another shower to cool down.

With a little effort, I managed to shimmy my way into the blouse this time. Once my arms had wiggled into the armholes I took a sigh of relief, but I couldn't manage to hook the buttons at the back despite my best efforts. I mentally delivered a hate speech to my tailor. My arms hurt too much as I struggled to fasten the blouse. This was such an embarrassing situation to be stuck in.

Harsh's sister had been getting ready in her mother's room all this while. She walked in as I was trying to hook the buttons. I had no option but to ask for her help.

I had seen such situations in several movies, a new bride who can't tie or untie something till her lustful husband comes to her rescue. It's all very romantic, until the husband is replaced by his sister and you have to hold your breath while she buttons you up on the count of three. What a tragedy!

It was late afternoon when I stepped on to the bus that was shuttling guests back and forth from the house to the venue. I finally ran into Harsh on the bus. He looked at me and smiled his irritating I-could-be-your-brother smile that exuded no charm, no romance and no sense of intimacy. I wished I could express my frustration without actually showing it. I wanted to convey my unhappiness to him but even to do that there needed to be some level of comfort between us. He just never made an effort. It's not as if Harsh was an unpleasant man. In fact, he was always polite and pleasant. It's just that when he looked at me, which happened rarely, it's as if I could be anybody to him—his mother, his uncle, a random person on the road. It didn't feel like I was special.

I had assumed that when two people, who have everything left to discover about each other, were going to get married, the relationship between them would be passionate and full of eagerness.

Even my parents after all these years had better chemistry than Harsh and me. And the problem wasn't just the lack of chemistry. It was as if Harsh didn't want any of it. Then why had he agreed to get married? This was not the bargain I had wanted to make. Was it too late to reconsider my decision?

22

278 days before the wedding

My family was finalizing the wedding date with the Tripathis and here I was, having second thoughts. The trip to Fatehabad had been an eye-opener, a warning, a glimpse into a life with Harsh's family, a peek into my future if I married him. I didn't want it. I didn't want to marry for the sake of crossing it off my bucket list. No, I couldn't. But what choice did I have? To upset my family when this clearly meant a great deal to them? They would never understand my situation, my point of view. I knew there was no point having this internal debate. I didn't possess the nerve to stall the chain of events that was in motion. I couldn't stand up to so many people. I couldn't bring myself to even discuss my apprehensions with anyone in the family.

At noon, the elders sat in the living room, discussing the wedding date. Harsh's father had given us two options. I would be married within the next three months.

I didn't know what to feel. I had longed for this, because I didn't know if it would ever happen. And now, the closer I was to getting married, the more I realized that this was not what I wanted. Life was short-changing me. What a nasty joke!

'Madhu, beta, come here,' Father called me.

I went to hear my fate, to know the date I would officially cease to be a fat burden on my family, the date of my wedding. Instead, I was received by frantic parents.

'Okay, your in-laws have called us over to discuss the wedding date. We are leaving. I think we will have lunch there. We should be back by evening.'

'Okay.'

'Your lunch is in the kitchen,' Mother said. 'Don't overeat.'

'Okay.'

'Let's hope all goes well.'

'Okay.'

Grandma was at her sister's house again. So I was home alone. I went back to my room and decided to take a nap. It was my quick fix for every problem. But ten minutes into my snooze, I was woken up by a phone call. I looked for my phone but found that it wasn't ringing.

I figured one of my parents must've left their phone behind. I dashed into the living room and managed to answer the call just in time. This call was about to change my life.

'Hello,' I answered the unknown number.

'Hi, good afternoon, may I speak to Mr Pandey?'

'This is his daughter speaking.'

'Oh, I was told this was his number.'

'It is, but he is not around at the moment. Can I pass on any message to him?'

'Yes, that would be great. Tell him Ravi Prasad had called to inform that the car is not available in red at the moment. There was a glitch at the manufacturing end so he was misinformed. The colour he wants to book will only be available at the end of the quarter. We are completely booked.'

I didn't immediately understand the context. The man was speaking gibberish. But it was not a wrong number. This person knew my father.

'I'm sorry I'm a bit confused. What is this regarding?'

'Oh. Ms Pandey, your father had come to our showroom to book the sports version of the new Amaze but he was insistent on delivery within forty-five days and wanted it only in red. Unfortunately, that is not possible. And . . .'

New? Car? Book? Red? What was he saying?

My breath caught in my chest. Before the salesman could finish his sentence, I had cut the line and didn't answer when he called again. It took me a moment to put two and two together. The realization was hard-hitting. There was no dramatic dropping of the phone, no collapsing to the ground in shock, just immobility and disbelief. A single moment of comprehension. As panic started to rise, I filled myself a glass of water and came back to the dining table. Anger built up inside me as my conviction grew firmer with every passing moment. I wanted to yell, but I gulped down the water in order to suppress the urge.

As I sat reflecting on what I had just found out, several things became clear. It is daunting when you discover something that has been lying in front of your eyes all along.

I thought about the relationship between Harsh's family and mine. And suddenly all the pieces started to fall in place. Their initial decision to meet me again, Harsh's easy acceptance in letting me pay the bill, the unexpected proposal, the diamond-studded gold ring for Harsh—could all this be related? The signs of their miserliness were there right from the beginning. *Good family, my foot!* Grandma's words resounded in my head. How could I have missed all this? The car that Harsh's family was bragging about was not being bought by them, IT WAS BEING BOUGHT BY MY FATHER! The Tripathis were out to milk my parents. They were making my father pay for my 'mistake' of being fat.

I can never describe how humiliated I felt at that moment. It was the final nail in the coffin. The incident that helped me arrive at a decision. Even if I had been looking forward to marrying Harsh, this was a deal-breaker. And the fact that I was anyway having second thoughts made it easier to take a decision. I tried to maintain my composure till my parents returned but I could feel anger radiating through my body. Restlessness would not let go of me. I wanted to confront my parents and I wanted to do it right then! How could they keep me in the dark about this? How could they even agree to do this? Was it so important to marry me off that they would pay for luxuries they could not even afford? Were they so doubtful of finding another man for me that they could not let go of Harsh regardless of the cost? It made me physically sick. I had been too quick to drink all that water. I vomited it out in a matter of seconds. This was beyond humiliating. One thought kept playing in my head. What if we were not buying them the car? Did my marriage depend on such perks? I was devastated.

I paced up and down in my house to steady my nerves. It was only a matter of minutes till my parents returned And then it would all be over. I had made up my mind to put an end to this episode. No matter what the repercussions, I was going to break off this engagement.

23

277 days before the wedding

Never had a gloomier morning dawned upon our house. The stillness of the house weighed heavy on all of us. The silence was deafening.

The previous evening, I had managed to wait until my parents showed up. They hadn't even properly set foot in the house, when I bombarded them with questions.

'How could you do this to me?' I yelled even as my mother was pulling the key out of the keyhole.

'What has happened?' Father asked worriedly as he removed his shoes. I was immobile and crying furiously.

Mother panicked.

'What has happened, Madhu? Is everything okay?' she rushed to me, dropping everything.

'You are paying them so that their son will marry me?' I sobbed. Even saying it out aloud filled me with disgust. My knees gave way and slowly I sank to the floor.

All my years of struggling with my body, the burden of carrying the identity of a fat girl, boiled down to this one moment. It was a complete breakdown. I held my face in my hands and cried like I had never cried before. This was no longer just about Harsh's family.

My father was rooted to the spot and Mother immediately hugged me.

'Who told you this?' she asked, trying to cradle my face but I fought her. I did not need her love at that moment, just her honesty.

I couldn't bring myself to speak. I just had to cry. I had to let it all out. Mother tried to approach me again but I pushed her away. It was beyond dramatic.

'Who told you this, Madhurima?'

'You still haven't answered me,' I yelled. 'This means it's true,' I shrieked in disbelief. 'I was still hoping it wasn't true. That I had somehow misunderstood the matter,' I said, covering my mouth in horror.

'How could you do this? How could you pay someone to marry me?'

'Don't talk rubbish,' Mother yelled. I looked for father. He had quietly retreated to the sofa and sat sombrely, his head in his hands. His reaction told me all that I needed to know. I was right.

'Just please don't talk to me ever again,' I screeched.

'Madhu, calm down. There is no need to behave like this.'

'How dare you tell me to calm down? You should be ashamed of yourselves.'

'We have not done anything to be ashamed of. We want the best for you and we will do our best to make it happen.'

'How blind can you be? Can you not see how wrong this is? Dowry is not legal. And that is not even your worst mistake. Have you no self-respect? Do you think I have no self-respect? I just . . . I can't even . . . How?'

'Please just relax, beta. Wash your face, then we will discuss the matter.'

'There is nothing left to discuss. As far as I'm concerned, this engagement or whatever the hell this nonsense was, it's over. Don't ever expect me to marry into a house like this. Ever.'

'Enough, Madhurima. Stop overreacting. I said we would discuss the matter.'

'And I said there is nothing to discuss. I will not marry Harsh. And if you force me I will leave this house, believe me,' I said with a note of finality. Father looked up in surprise. Our eyes met. Before I could approach him, he hung his head again.

'What is your problem, Madhu? Why are you making this so difficult for us? After everything we are doing.'

I stared at my mother in disbelief. There was no point discussing this any further. She and I were on opposite ends of the spectrum in this matter. I turned to my father. It was he in whom I was most disappointed.

'How could you let all this happen, Papa?' I asked, the trauma of betrayal evident in my voice. He could not meet my eyes. His head was in his hands, tears falling silently on his knees.

'I did not expect this from you,' I said, hoping to sound as disappointed as I was.

After that, the house became still. I locked myself in my room for the rest of the night and I think my parents did the same. My mother understood that this was not the right time to talk to me so she let me be. I lay awake for most of the night, unable to believe all that had happened in the last few months since I had agreed to get married.

More slowly than ever, morning arrived but I wasn't ready to face the day. Mother was in for a rude shock if she had hoped that I had sobered down. My anger had not subsided. I was still in shock So when she came to discuss the matter, I shot her down.

'Will you tell the Tripathis that the wedding is off or should I?' I asked confidently.

'Madhu, please, beta. You're my mature and understanding daughter,' Mother said. What do parents think when they use such childish tricks to pacify you?

'No, Ma. I'm your stupid and thick-headed one. You're wasting your time if you think I'm going to change my mind. I could never marry a man who would take money from my parents in exchange for marrying me. I would rather die alone.'

'Madhu! Don't say such things. And stop exaggerating. We have not paid anyone to marry you. Can a father not gift his daughter something at her wedding?'

How could I not have laughed at this one!

'Please, Ma,' I snorted. 'Don't even try that one. You know as well as I do that this was no gift. Why would they claim to be buying the car if it were a gift? Why would Papa hide this from me when he can't even select a keychain without consulting me? At least make sure your story adds up before lying to me.'

'Nobody is lying to you. Yes, we didn't tell you. Because we knew what your reaction would be. And you've proved us right.'

'Too bad then that I found out.'

'Madhu, I know you are upset. But . . .'

'Upset? I'm embarrassed. I'm ashamed. I'm so many things that I don't deserve to be. All because of you. How dare you give anybody the right to demean me like this? I'm just so embarrassed.'

'But why? This is normal. Everyone gives the boy's side some expensive thing or another. What is so wrong with a gift?'

'Giving a gift is very different from fulfilling a demand. Look at me and tell me that this was not a prerequisite for our marriage.'

'No, it's not like you're making it sound.'

'You're lying.'

'I'm not.'

'So when was it decided that we would be buying them a car? And what else have they demanded from us?'

'Look, Madhu, that is between Papa and Harsh's father. I don't know what or how it was all decided. They wanted a new car and Papa decided to buy it for them. That's all.'

'You're twisting it all. You're making it sound like it's okay but it is not. It all fits now. It makes sense. I knew something was not right. There were signs all along. Why was there a diamond in Harsh's ring? We never buy diamonds. It's Papa's policy. Always invest in gold.'

'Because rules don't apply when your daughter is getting married. For you, Papa and I will do anything.'

'I appreciate that, mom. But it still doesn't change the fact that this is wrong. The fact that it was hidden from me proves that even you know it is wrong.'

'So if we had told you about the gift it would have been okay?'

'No, then I would have stopped you right then. It is so demeaning that they have such conditions for accepting me.'

'And I am telling you it was not a condition. Madhu, in life every situation is not black or white. There are grey shades. That does not make people bad. I know you are hurt because we hid it from you but . . .'

'No, mom, it's not just that. It's their double-standard attitude that is bothering me. Why did they not mention that it was a gift in front of me? They want to take the credit of splurging on the wedding but want us to pay the bills. As a gift, I would accept it, but a gift has to be given out of free will. This is a demand. I know it.'

'But what's the difference?'

'Oh, it makes all the difference. As a gift, it is acceptable, as a condition it is not. It means that had Papa not been able to buy the car and whatever else he is giving them, then there would have been no marriage. I can't let someone walk all over my self-respect like this. I am sure this would not have happened if Harsh were marrying someone like Ragini or Anu. But it's okay. If they can't accept me as I am then they don't have to accept me at all.'

'But they are accepting you.'

'So if you tell them that you cannot give the car, will there still be a wedding?'

'Enough, Madhu. Why are you getting involved in matters that don't concern you? Just enjoy this phase. We are there to do the worrying.'

'Matters that don't concern me? Are you kidding, mom? I have to go and live with those people. Every damn thing concerns me. And what enjoy? Have you seen the excuse of a man that Harsh is? Do you really think I would be happy with an ugly loser like him?'

Mother was silent.

'No woman would. And you know it. But no. You're just grateful that some person with male organs has decided that he will put an end to your embarrassment of being the mother of an unmarried fat girl, so no matter what the price is, quite literally, you will not let go of this opportunity to get rid of your daughter. Who knows when such a deal will come again, right?'

'What nonsense you talk! Making us sound like monsters. You just don't know how much we love you and what we could do for you.'

'Then do this much for me. Call this wedding off.'

'You just won't listen, will you? It's best you talk to your father about this.'

'Oh, I would love that. I would love to see whether he has the courage to face me.'

'He did nothing wrong. We only have your best interest in mind.'

'Right. And tomorrow when the new red car becomes old and they start harassing you for more money and ill-treating me, then what will you do?'

'Nothing like that will happen. Believe me.'

'How can you be so sure? How can even the slightest chance of that happening not make you want to stop this? You wouldn't do this if you had my best interests in mind.'

'Beta, you're over-thinking this. It's not as bad as you're making it seem. Yes, it was our fault not telling you. But why should you make them pay for it?'

'Them pay for it? They are not paying for anything. That's the whole problem. They are misers. I should have figured it out in the beginning. Why was there no diamond in my ring?'

'Because you hate diamonds! Isn't that true?'

'Yes, but that's not the reason I didn't get one. They are stingy. And that would still be okay with me if they weren't milking my parents just because they think they are compromising by accepting a fat bride.'

'I think your grandmother should deal with you now. Maybe she can talk some sense into you,' Mother said. It was a good move. Grandma could take me down in any debate. I was thrown a little off balance. But I was not done standing up for myself. No one could bully me into this. My Achilles', heel had been exposed so offensively that I could not think of forgiving my parents for this, ever. My shortcoming was a point of trade in the marriage market. Was there a rate card? Ten lakh rupees for every ten kg in excess, payable in cash or kind. Red-colour cars preferable. The thought made my stomach roil.

'Beta, what will we do if this rishta breaks? How will we ever find a good eligible boy once the news spreads in the community, in society? It will be a dead end for us,' Mother said, crying, as if her life depended on it. Maybe it did. Maybe this meant a lot more to my family than I'd reckoned. But it still didn't justify going behind my back and allowing such a deal to take place.

On at least three occasions, I wondered if I was overreacting but then I would think of Harsh, a man earning enough to afford any luxury he wanted and my decision would be planted even more firmly. I wondered what and how many more conditions had been placed by Harsh's family that I didn't know of.

'Just please leave my room,' I said, being ruder than I'd ever been to my mother. Reluctantly, she left.

24

269 days before the wedding

Have you ever seen a family in mourning after someone's death? Multiply that atmosphere by ten. That's the state of a family when a daughter's marriage is called off. Everyone perpetually looks like they are on the verge of tears. Smiling is illegal, voices are hushed, faces are serious, food is tasteless and enjoyment, what's that?

The engagement had been broken. Harsh and I were no longer an item. Had we ever been one to begin with? I don't think so. I had a more romantic relationship with my neighbour's snobbish cat than I'd had with Harsh. And I hate cats. How had I managed this mammoth task of calling it quits? Well, you've got to do what you've got to do. You've got to stand up for yourself before it gets too late. I had no choice but to make sure it was done.

In the two days that followed the crucial confrontation with my parents, several arguments took place in my house. Voices were raised, warnings were given and pleas were made. My mother actually begged me to comply, to go through with this marriage on two occasions, but I did not budge.

I knew little of the dialogue between my parents and Harsh's at that point. I was ignoring my parents as much as it was possible to ignore someone you live with. Father avoided me completely. I think he was too embarrassed to face me. Mother attempted to reconcile but every time she asked me to reconsider my decision, I would ask her to leave.

The atmosphere at home had never been this hostile. However, while overhearing conversations from behind my door, I had figured that my father had managed to put on hold the matter of the wedding date for now. My parents had been hoping that Grandma would be able to change my mind but she couldn't. Arguing with her was like banging your head on a wall so I didn't talk to her at all. Eventually, they had to tell the Tripathis that the wedding was off. I don't know how they went about this task and I never bothered to ask. It didn't matter.

The next morning, Harsh's mother came home and gave my family an earful. For the few minutes that she rumbled, she stood at the entrance of our house, saying that she would never set foot inside. I heard the first few minutes of her rant diligently. She spoke at length about Harsh being out of my league, of them doing this as a favor given our good reputation. She then went on about how Harsh had rejected several girls who were fit to be queens. She predicted I would never be able to find a great boy like her son. My apologetic parents heard her monologue without a single retort.

You'd think hearing all this would have made my blood boil, but it didn't. I was indifferent to the spectacle.

I had taken indefinite leave from work citing a family emergency—this was one by all means! I spent the next couple of days holed up in my room, coming out only when necessary.

I would order at least one burger a day and eat it in bed as I reflected on Harsh's lack of self-respect. Burgers were my official Depression Food. I gained more than three kilos in less than a week, washing away all the hard work of the past few months.

For the first two days, I hadn't thought of Harsh at all. I was still recovering from what my parents had done. Once that sank in, I started thinking about him while drowning in self-pity. To be honest, I didn't feel as let down by him as I did by others. He had never given me a reason to expect anything from him to begin with. I always had a weird feeling about him. He was just . . . off, odd, weird. It helped that there was no romantic emotion between us. Breaking the engagement was easy. An emotional bond between two people needs more than just the sliding of a ring and that too such a stupid one! I had removed it and kept it on the dining table the morning after the humiliating discovery.

News of the wedding being called off reached Anu. I had been avoiding her calls and messages so she had rung up my mother. And that's how she learnt that the wedding was off. Her following messages revealed that Mother hadn't told her the reason. She inquired several times but I could not bring myself to respond. It was easy for me to ignore her but my family could not afford to ignore anybody.

Society makes people feel answerable to it. My parents were interrogated by a number of irrelevant people—neighbours, friends, distant relatives. Even our neighbour's housekeeper offered us her sympathies!

Everyone claimed to be a well-wisher but they were only scrounging for gossip. Some wanted to know if the hunt for another groom had begun. The condoling chats always ended with famous proverbs. 'Whatever happens, happens for the best', this one defeated others by a decent margin. 'Time heals everything' was a close runner-up.

It would take a long time for my family to recover from this setback. They just needed to stop thinking of it as one.

25

255 days before the wedding

I had to get out of the house. I just had to. I had started going to work again and had even begun attending lectures. I needed an outing, a change of scene, fresh air. The frigid atmosphere at home had started to thaw. The mourning was coming to an end. Although my parents were still avoiding contact with the outside world, they had resumed their daily routine. Grandma was back to her kitty parties. She was the most headstrong among us. It was she who restored normalcy at home. Grandma was a paradox; she was the most conservative and the most modern member of our family. And I am grateful to her for helping me move on by just being normal.

Sometimes, the best help that someone can offer is just letting you be.

I knew it was only a matter of time before my parents started thinking about my marriage again. For them, the task of finding a groom had only toughened. But it would take them a while to approach me with this topic.

Our relationship had become strained in the past couple of days. The knots, however, started to loosen. For the first few days, I avoided everyone. I purposely got out of my room when no one was in the living room, usually before or after everyone had had breakfast. The food would be kept on the kitchen counter for me. I would quickly gobble it, then get ready and leave only to return after the rest of the family had retired to their respective rooms. A week must have passed like that. And then slowly, we stopped avoiding each other. I would be in the same room with them but not make eye contact. The next step in the road to recovery was giving information. 'I'll be late tonight,' I would say while leaving for office in the morning. 'Your dinner is in the oven,' mom would say when I came back from college. Generic communication had begun. Papa and I still hadn't spoken. On the other hand, Grandma and I were absolutely fine.

One morning, mom came to my room and asked, 'What will you have for dinner?' This question, after a period of fighting and avoiding each other, was a sign that things were back to normal. It was time to call a truce. We had all suffered enough. With mom, it was obvious that matters would straighten out. She and I had had fights before and survived. It was my equation with Father that I was worried about. Have you ever been in a situation where the most important person in your life has hurt you and only he can help you overcome the pain?

That was my state. I had always been my daddy's girl. At this point in my life, I needed him to be there with me and not against me. I needed him to tell me that it was okay not to be able to find a suitable groom. I needed him to tell me that even if no man accepted me he would never leave my side. I needed him to tell me that my decision was right even though I had gone against him. I needed him. And I knew that he needed me too.

A few days later, Mother approached me again and it looked as if she had something serious to discuss. This was definitely not her 'will-you-eat-*bhindi*' face.

Before I could guess what the matter was, Mother came around the bed and hugged me. I had no idea why I was being smothered in my dear mother's bosom, but the gesture touched me. Out of nowhere, I began to cry and so did she. It had been hard for us to be on opposite ends for so long. Mother's warmth, her proximity, her love made me a little girl again. For those few moments, I was transported back in time—when being fat had actually been my USP.

'I'm so sorry, my beta,' she said holding me tight. 'I'm so sorry for what you have had to go through.'

'You are right. We should never have agreed to marry you off to such a family. They don't deserve you. We were so blind,' she sniffed.

I remained quiet, relieved that I was finally being understood.

'Since this chapter has begun, you've had to go through so many difficult situations. My brave girl. I'm so sorry for not trying to understand you.'

'Okay, Mumma, I can't breathe,' I said breaking away from her. 'Now stop crying and let me go.'

'No,' she said, bosom-smothering me tighter.

'Uff! Please, Mumma. Stop being filmy now,' I said, tearing her from me. All this clingy, emotional business with my mother always made me uncomfortable.

She eventually sat on the bed, making it clear that we weren't done yet.

'Beta, listen. Papa is very disturbed because of what has happened. He is not even eating properly. I know he should come and talk to you but he is too embarrassed. He feels it is his fault. But the truth is that it was because of me and your Nani that all this happened. We were the ones who convinced Papa to accept all their demands.'

So finally we were on the same page. The car was not a gift; it was a demand.

'Don't worry, mom. I'll talk to him.'

'Actually, don't talk to him about this. I don't want him to feel guiltier. You can already see how sorry he is. Why bring up this subject at all? Instead, I was thinking why don't we all go out for dinner tonight? It has been such a long time since we went out together. We will go to any place you like. I want us to become normal again. I want my house to have a happy atmosphere again.'

'Should I make a reservation for 9 p.m. then?' I said sportingly. Finally, I could see a silver lining. Oh, how badly had I wanted my family to be with me in this!

Mother smiled as she rose from the bed. Before leaving, she turned and said, 'Oh, and one more thing, beta. Papa, Nani and I have decided that there is no hurry to get you married. Even if you are, we are not ready to part with you just yet,' she said endearingly.

I could not believe my ears. How could I not hold my pillow and cry after she left? I was officially free from the wedding circus.

26

215 days before the wedding

It was time for my fourth dance class that evening.

I'd walked into the first one feeling extremely nervous about shaking my body next to other people shaking their bodies!

My body was not an asset for me. You know this. And to groove it skilfully to music, while several people watched me was not something I looked forward to, but I had decided to give it a shot.

Anu had assured me that this teacher was really good. She was back in my life. After retreating into a shell for several weeks, when I finally decided to come out of it, it was Anu I contacted first. She had tried her best to be there for me during the most unpleasant phase of my life but I had blocked her out completely. Sometimes you need your friends to tide you over rough times, but sometimes you need to do it alone. We caught up over drinks one night and I filled her in on all that had happened. Oh, did I mention earlier that I was into drinking now? Isn't that what you're supposed to do after a break-up? I'm a fast learner.

Since our first night out, Anu and I had been meeting regularly every ten days for drinks and dinner. She would come down to her parents' house more often than I'd expected and it was a delight to meet her every now and then.

Life was back to normal even though it could not be as simple as it used to be. The truth was my confidence had taken a major hit since the whole debacle. If I had earlier been conscious of my body, now I was unable to deal with it. And to add to my woes, I was eating like a hungry pig on the loose. It was Anu who suggested I do some activity to let off steam. She said whenever she was stressed out (what the hell did she have to be stressed about?) she would take dance classes to take her mind off problems. You could guess how desperately I needed help if I was considering joining a dance class!

I was in the last leg of my MBA course. There were no more lectures so I had enough time to devote to a hobby. Self-conscious and wary, I felt like a misfit, surrounded by a group of talented, sexy and fit dancers on day one of the jazz dance class. Apart from me, there were three men and eight women, of whom one was fat. The rest were seasoned dancers and dressed in tights, sports bras, cut-out tops, vests—basically anything that accentuated their toned bodies.

I lurked around in the back row, dressed in track pants and my father's T-shirt, trying my best to stay hidden from the instructor, a middle-aged man with a sculpted body. Of course, I had a crush on him.

The second class was not very different from the first—both were equally disastrous. The third was not very different from the second. I would get tired and breathless faster than the rest of the lot. Within minutes of the commencement of the class, I would have sweat patches in questionable areas of my body. The exercises were painful and I would give up halfway. Remembering the choreography was a huge struggle for me as was the fast pace of the class.

At the end of the third class, I came home exhausted and ready to abandon this newfound passion of mine. It only seemed to be getting tougher. The next morning, even a mild sneeze hurt my sore body. I had made up my mind I would not go.

However, on the evening of my fourth class, when Grandma said she would be dropping me to class since she was heading to a new beauty parlour nearby, I could not talk myself out of it. I didn't want to tell her that I was planning to discontinue the classes because I was no good. I couldn't think of a way to talk myself out of it so I went with her. Unfortunately, I was in for a terrible surprise when I reached.

The usual routine had been called off that day. Instead, every student was supposed to perform an impromptu SOLO jig for the others. This was to build confidence, ironically. I wanted to run right out of the studio but didn't have the courage to even do that.

The class began and the first girl went up to do her bit. It would be only a few minutes before they called out my name. It was terrifying. I decided to leave on the pretext of falling sick but the other fat girl got to the instructor with the trick first. Sadly, he saw through her move. She was asked to stay, her sudden sickness notwithstanding. Such tyranny! I thought I'd vomit if I had to go through this. Making a complete arse of myself in front of so many gorgeous men and women, with nothing to camouflage me—yikes! I sat there watching my classmates deliver one good performance after another, dreading the two minutes when I would be the centre of attention and cursing Anu for talking me into this.

'Madhurima, right?' the instructor announced, looking at me. I considered not responding. 'Go on, you're next. Don't be shy or nervous. We're all dancers here.'

'I . . . I . . . can't. Please. Maybe next time,' I offered. This would never be since I did not intend to ever come back.

'No, no. There's no need to feel conscious. There's no right or wrong in dance. Just enjoy yourself. Come on. We're waiting.'

'Come on!' one of the girls said.

'You'll be awesome,' one of the guys said. If only he hadn't been so good-looking, this would have been a lot easier. I didn't move for as long as it is possible to stay immobile when all eyes are on you. Eventually, it didn't seem like I could get out of this one.

Shakily, I rose to my feet and took centre stage. *What's the worst that can happen? They will laugh at me. They will think I'm ridiculous. Hardly matters,* I consoled myself. I would never have to see them again. I wasn't coming back.

They played some song I did not recognize and I froze.

'Just start moving. Do anything,' the instructor suggested.

Anything, anything, anything, I said to myself. For some reason, I started to jump on the spot. Maybe I had forgotten this was a dance class?

'That's good, that's good,' the instructor said. Maybe he too had forgotten that this was a dance class? People started to clap and I don't know why this irritated me. It was nice of them to not laugh at me but I didn't want their encouragement. I wanted their admiration.

After thirty seconds of being a bouncy ball, I decided to stop. This was a nightmare.

'Okay, never mind,' the instructor offered. 'Good attempt,' he said like a true teacher should, despite my clumsiness. He was about to pick the next student when I decided that this was not how I wanted to come across in front of the class. The image of a scared, nervous, fat girl would never change if I didn't erase the impression I had created. They had seen my worst already. I decided to give it another go.

'Umm . . . can you change the track?' I asked, surprising everyone in the class.

'Sure. Anything in particular?' the instructor said, excited all of a sudden.

'Uh . . . just any Salman Khan song.'

He chuckled as everyone grew curious and I felt like I was about to faint. Then I heard the beats of *O O Jaane Jaana* from the popular movie *Pyar Kiya Toh Darna Kya* and instinctively closed my eyes, glad that this was the song chosen for my comeback. *I've got this.* Slowly, forgetting about the others, I started to groove.

Gently grooving to the music with closed eyes, I pictured that I was a model—long hair, flat stomach, longer legs. And I owned the stage. I started to enjoy the beat as the familiar words kicked in. And suddenly from the graceful model, I turned into a boisterous man who didn't give two hoots about what the world thought. I shut my eyes tighter and let my body take over. I knew the lyrics perfectly and danced without thinking of my next move. I could hear people cheering but tried to block them all out. I told myself that there was no one present except me. Trying to recall the trademark steps, I danced and danced and danced. A hand strike in the air, a pelvic thrust to the side, a hip roll here, a slight shimmy there and before I knew it, the song ended.

'Superrrrrb!' clapped the other fat girl. When I opened my eyes she was smiling at me, clearly impressed. She had never before been so pumped up in class. I had motivated her. Everybody cheered. She was next. I was red in the face and out of breath.

'Why the hell were you so hesitant? You're a great dancer,' came an astonished voice. 'Try our Bollywood classes. And next time—eye contact,' said my instructor, patting me on the back and nudging me to the side. I couldn't believe it was over! This was by all means a big achievement for me.

From that day on, I had a newfound motivation to go to the dance class. Because of one little push, one sign of progress, my attitude had changed. Someone in the class looked up to me now, just as I looked up to all those fit dancers. Suddenly, the class seemed to be getting easier or rather, I seemed to be getting better. I could keep up with the warm-up routine, I could recall eighty per cent of the choreography and I could improvise moves for the parts I didn't remember.

I was no longer just the fat girl in class, I was the dark horse.

27

180 days before the wedding

My graduation ceremony was held the previous week. I was now officially an MBA. I sat looking at my pictures from the felicitation ceremony, which was attended by my proud parents. They looked truly happy in the photographs—something I had not felt they would be for a long time after I broke off the engagement. If they were still not over it, they were doing a good job at hiding it.

Mother had printed out some of the photographs and entrusted me with the task of adding them to the album comprising pictures from my school and college days.

Mother had a record of every accomplishment of mine—big and small. There were pictures of me when I topped the crafts class, got the second prize in a 100-metre race—can you imagine that I could run? As I flipped through the album, I noticed how my age and weight climbed up simultaneously. From a skinny kid, I had turned into a ball. Luckily, there wasn't a noticeable change in weight in the photos of my graduation from senior college and those of my post-graduation. The graph was now stagnant. At least I could call myself well-maintained.

I had my newfound love for dance classes to thank for the few kilos I had shed in the last two months and that too without putting in too much effort. Strange, isn't it? A few months ago, I was killing myself to lose weight and it just wouldn't happen. And now that I had stopped obsessing over it, it was taking care of itself.

As I sat browsing through a few more photo albums, stored in the one mammoth cupboard that housed all such albums, it dawned on me how physically active I used to be as a young girl. In fact, to say that dance was my newfound passion was wrong. It was a rekindled one. There were so many photographs of me in skating classes, skipping on a jump rope, playing badminton with my dad.

And then there were pictures of that one summer when I got really fat. I wish there was a tragic story behind my rapid widening. For years, I wished I could have something to blame, like a medical condition that makes you fat. It would take away the guilt, the shame. It would provide me with a comeback for the several comments and observations that people made initially. Someone would say, 'You've put on quite a bit of weight,' and I wished I had some concrete reason to give like, 'Oh aunty, I've been diagnosed with overeatingandnoexcersizonia.' And then they would sympathize with me. They would understand that I was not really fat, it was not my fault and it was to be blamed on something else. They would understand that it was okay for me to be fat, that actually I was thin but due to this serious condition I had put on weight. But unfortunately, that wasn't the case. I had only my laziness and love of overeating during that beautiful summer to blame for my fit-to-fat transformation.

It wasn't that I had inflated like a balloon. The gain was gradual. After gaining the first ten kilos, things went downhill or rather up-scale. Sadly, pun intended.

The timing didn't help because I was in the last two years of high school, which meant I was engrossed in studies and tuitions. All physical activities, like the occasional swimming session, the summer holiday hobby classes, the dance classes, took a back seat. Eating was my favourite and only way to cope at that point. I didn't look at it as a problem. I thought with time I would be able to get rid of the weight as easily as I had acquired it. Over those two years, my personality (and my wardrobe) automatically changed. Due to the weight gain, my favourite clothes stopped fitting me. Vests had been replaced by loose T-shirts, tights had been replaced by baggy pants, (sometimes you choose the tomboy life, sometimes the tomboy life chooses you) my stamina plunged, outdoor games were replaced by electronic ones and soon I began college.

There was no looking back after that. College life consumed me as I consumed everything consumable in sight. By the time my weight gain truly started to bother me, the damage had been done. The 'fat brigade' had accepted me as one of its own. The label stuck. Then adult life happened and here I was.

Looking at the photographs after such a long time made me think: had I not been such a reckless eater that summer, would my story have been different?

28

163 days before the wedding

Anu had called me over to her mum's place for dinner. It did occur to me that she was staying over at her parents' house a bit too frequently. That day I learnt the reason behind it.

'I'm . . . I'm not happy,' she said, sobbing as we sat down on her bed eating wafers. 'I know, I know . . . it doesn't look like that, it shouldn't be like that. But it is.'

Anu, the perfect girl living the perfect life with the perfect man, was saying that she wasn't happy? How could it be? Maybe she was mistaken. She was probably PMSing.

'What has happened?' I asked, totally at bay regarding the problem.

'I can't do this. Maybe marriage is not for me,' she said.

At first, I was stunned. I had not anticipated that there was already trouble in paradise. I could not stop thinking of her grand wedding as she launched into her sob story. In the next one hour I got to know everything.

Everything went well in the first few months of Anu's marriage, the famous 'honeymoon phase'. She didn't even realize when or how the problems started to crop up. It wasn't long after they had come back from the honeymoon that the cracks began to appear. The main problem was frequent misunderstandings with the in-laws. There was no real issue between Akshay and her but, at a crossroads, Akshay always favoured his parents. This started giving rise to fights between the newly-weds.

'I'm so sick of that house that "I", Anu Sharma, actually started looking for a job,' she said, stressing on how much of a big deal this was. Anu never wanted to take up a job after marriage. She wanted to have a baby soon and then maybe design clothes.

'And they have a problem with that also. Because apparently I "never showed an inclination to work" earlier. *Arre*! Can't a person change her mind?'

'I tell you, marriages are all jokes! Nothing is as it seems,' she continued.

I barely spoke during her rant, drinking in this unimaginable scenario.

'Sorry, I don't mean to scare you. I'm sure you will have a happy marriage whenever you marry,' she said, wiping her nose.

'Stop crying, Anu. Don't be one of those dramatic wives. If you have a problem, solve it. I know Akshay loves you. He's always so nice to you.'

'All that doesn't matter when there is a new fight every day. Love goes out of the window. Peace is the most important thing in a household.'

After that, Anu narrated each incident in detail whenever Akshay had sided with his parents and I sat quietly as her sounding board.

I left after dinner.

That night I was ashamed of myself, not because I was unable to offer any good advice to Anu, but because in spite of what she was going through, I didn't feel bad for her. As mean as it might make me sound, the bitter truth was that I was sadistically comforted. Before you judge me, I hope I can convey just how much I love Anu. She was and will always be my best friend. But, you see, while growing up, I had always felt like her shadow. Boys wanted to be with her, girls wanted to be like her. I was the imperfect one in our pair. You know the quintessential nerdy, bespectacled, loveless girl in every teen movie? I was she, except I wasn't even smart or intelligent (or bespectacled). I was just the fat girl. And all my years of playing second fiddle to Anu had built up to that one moment when I saw something not working out for her.

For the first time I saw Anu as just another person, who was suffering like others were, who was as imperfect as others were, who couldn't handle something as others couldn't. Suddenly, she was not above me, I was not below her like how I had always believed I was. Suddenly I had company. I was not alone in this struggle called 'life'.

Of course, I never wanted anything bad to happen to her. Never. But when I saw imperfection in her life, I didn't feel bad, felt terrible about not feeling bad.

Human emotions are complicated. Humans are complicated.

29

159 days before the wedding

My grandma's social butterfly image meant that she had many a gathering to attend. Although her circle was not very big, it was more active than those of people half her age. Be it the launch of a new restaurant or the shutting down of an old one, Grandma's circle of fellow septuagenarians was always ready to explore the city. They weren't very extravagant but knew how to enjoy themselves. From playing cards to watching the latest movies, the women, mostly single or widows, had an agenda set for at least two days of the week.

Turn-by-turn, Father and I often dropped and picked Grandma up from her get-togethers, if the location was convenient for chauffeuring.

That morning, she was busy setting her hair in hot rollers as early as 10 a.m. for a lunch party that she had to attend. Grandma had extraordinary patience in decking up for her gatherings. But to be fair, the lunch was being hosted by Meenu aunty, whose parties were touted as being the best organized, with innovative games, delicious food and novel return gifts. Meenu aunty had the slimmest figure and the fattest bank account in the group. She had acted in a lesser-known south Indian movie in her youth, which earned her the title of a 'celebrity' in her clique. She was the undisputed 'IT girl' of the group—a position my grandma had been eyeing for a while. Of course, Grandma had to look her best at this luncheon.

'So which one of you is driving me to that attention-seeking Meenu's house?' she asked during breakfast, hot rollers covering the entire length of her thinning hair, nails properly filed, eyebrows non-existent.

Father looked at me in response to her query—a smart move. I knew Meenu aunty's house wasn't nearby; I had gone there once to pick Grandma up. Father usually chauffeured her on weekdays but it was a holiday; either of us could do it.

I had to play it as smartly as Father, which meant not refusing Grandma directly. So, I looked pointedly at Mother, passing the buck on to her. Household politics, I tell you!

'Ma, why don't you just take a cab?' my mother suggested softly, avoiding Grandma's eyes, pretending to be busy applying butter on her toast.

'A CAB!' Grandma exclaimed, eyes popping out, hand on her chest as if she would get a cardiac arrest any moment.

Silence followed.

'You want me to take a cab to that Meenakshi's house? Is that what my life has come to? Three grown-up children and not one to take the old woman out! Oh, if it weren't for my aching knees I would have driven myself.'

For the record, Grandma didn't know how to drive. She claimed to have driven a lot in her youth and had a photograph in the driver's seat of our deceased Ambassador as proof. But legend has it that she was only posing. According to Mother, Grandma had tried driving twice and banged the car on both occasions.

Had it not been Meenu aunty's house, she would've been perfectly fine with going in a cab.

'Fine, I'll take you,' I said, confident that the reluctance in my voice would make her feel guilty and suggest that she go on her own.

'Great. We'll leave by noon,' she said quickly and sipped her tea.

A little after noon, Grandma stepped out of her room dressed in a light blue maxi dress that, thankfully, didn't reveal her figure. She would've looked fine had it not been for the ridiculous, colourful hat on her head, her favourite, which she maintained was high fashion.

I was to drive her and her friend, Guddi aunty, to the lunch and Guddi aunty's son would pick them up later. They take you to kindergarten, you take them to kitty parties, that is the deal.

It took about an hour to reach Meenu aunty's house. I wasn't very familiar with the roads in that part of the city; we didn't go there often.

On my way back, I was waiting at a red light when someone caught my attention on the opposite side of the road. A man was walking out of a building and going towards a car. It was Harsh.

All this while, he may have crossed my mind occasionally but I hadn't been curious about his whereabouts. I had managed to forget about him easily, but now that I had seen him, I wanted to know what he was up to.

Before I could decide what to do, Harsh had already reversed the car out of the parking spot and was heading into one of the by-lanes. By the time the light turned green, he was out of sight. I quickly changed lanes to follow him but couldn't spot his car. I knew he didn't live too far away. I contemplated heading towards his house but then another idea struck me.

About five minutes later, I entered the building that my ex-fiancé had just left. I had never been this snoopy. It was exciting. I was about to find out something big, I could feel it in the air. Finding him in the middle of nowhere was no coincidence. Fate wanted me to discover something— the hidden wife, the illegitimate child, something that would add everything up and make Harsh's aloofness, his far-from-regular-behaviour valid, acceptable and understandable. Or maybe his marriage had been arranged to someone else now. And that someone else lived here. The possibilities were driving me crazy.

I entered the building as casually as a regular visitor would, but was stopped by the watchman. I saw the board of a dental clinic behind him and lied that I was here to visit the doctor.

'But he isn't at the clinic today,' the watchman said in Hindi.

Realizing that I would need his help in figuring out why Harsh was here, I decided to give it up. As confident as a wife spying on her husband, I inquired which apartment the man in the grey shirt had gone to in the building. The watchman was a little taken aback and understood that he was in an advantageous position here.

'Can't give out details,' he said righteously.

I thought a sweetener might make him talk so I took out a fifty-rupee note and fiddled around with it as I repeated my question. The watchman didn't divulge any information although I swear he looked as if he would lunge at the note any minute. I badgered him a little to open his mouth but he didn't give in, clearly enjoying this.

Ignoring his protests, I went inside the building but there was no knowing which flat Harsh had visited. The building was a regular residential establishment, which offered no clue. Feeling a bit foolish, I decided to give up the pointless quest.

How did it matter anyway? It was a stupid idea. There could be innumerable reasons as to why Harsh had come here, like dropping his grandmother to a kitty party!

I quietly walked out of the building. I must not have taken more than three steps when the watchman came out running, seeing his baksheesh slipping away.

'Listen madam, because you seem like a genuine person I will help you out,' he said, as if he were doing this only for me.

I wanted to act pricey this time but wanted his help more than that.

'Okay,' I said, folding my hands, expecting an answer.

He rubbed his left palm with his right thumb making it clear that his lips were sealed till he received a tip. I quickly took out the fifty again and, thankfully, he accepted it without any more fuss.

'Now tell me, why had that man come here?'

'He comes here to meet the doctor,' informed the watchman, checking the note against the sunlight.

What a waste of effort! The last person to give me some juicy insight into Harsh's life would be his dentist. I didn't want any details of how Harsh's gums were. This was a closed chapter in my life and I should have let it remain one, except one thing gnawed at me as I was making my way to the car for the second time.

I turned and shouted, 'But you said the doctor isn't in the clinic today.'

'Not him. The one behind the building,' the watchman said and walked back inside.

My curiosity was piqued again. Of course, I turned around but, this time, I circled the building to get to the backside.

As I inched closer to Harsh's big secret, if any, I wondered whether my opinion of him would change if I discovered something earth-shattering, like a cancer specialist or a fertility clinic. I knew I was being overdramatic but well, it runs in the family.

However, I was in for a rude shock when I found what I was looking for. Even in all my wild conclusions, I had not thought of this.

In front of me was a signboard that read: Dr Balwinder Marwah, MBBS, MD (Psychiatry).

I stood rooted to the spot. A shiver ran down my spine. A psychiatrist? A PSYCHIATRIST? WHAT! Had I almost married a madman? A lunatic, a sociopath, a schizophrenic? I went through the list of all the people who I reckoned went to psychiatrists. The revelation was totally unexpected.

I recalled my interactions with Harsh for a clue. There was something off about him from the beginning, but I didn't imagine it to be so dark, so heavy. A psychiatrist? It just wouldn't sink in. And we all thought I was the flawed one.

I didn't know what to do next.

Was this a sign that the break-up was a blessing in disguise? Had I dodged a bullet by ridding myself of a deranged man with a gory past and a troublesome future? Was fate helping me move on from what I had been through? The shame, the embarrassment, the unending inquisition, the sorry state of my parents. Was I just supposed to rejoice the fact that I wasn't the faulty one? Was this my cue to run straight out and never turn back? *Or should I give in to my curiosity and meddle just a little, inquire just a little more about what exactly Harsh's problem was?*

I went into the clinic, pretending that I needed to see the doctor urgently, but the receptionist shot me down.

'Doctor only take half-day today. Please come with appointment.'

'But . . .'

'Doctor only take half-day today. Please come with appointment.'

The third time she repeated it, I felt like punching her in the face. At least then we'd have proof that I needed anger management. Could that be the reason why Harsh came here? Anger management? But then I could not imagine him as someone with a wild temper. In fact, I had always thought he was too docile, too cold. Hell, he hadn't even bothered to contact me since the marriage had been called off. Who does that?

I had to halt spying for the time being. I would take an appointment and return at the earliest. I had to unravel the mystery of the man I had almost married.

30

156 days before the wedding

'Hello, Ms Pandey. Please take a seat,' Dr Marwah, soft-spoken and kind-eyed, said as he shuffled through some papers.

'Hello, doctor,' I walked in and sat on the 'patient's chair', a small, comfortable sofa.

'I hear you've been quite insistent on an immediate appointment. My secretary tells me she had no choice but to squeeze you in because you called her repeatedly.'

I smiled guiltily. I had found out that my ex-fiancé—the only man I'd ever been involved with (if we can just pretend for a while that what Harsh and I had had was 'being involved') was seeing a psychiatrist. Of course I was going to pester his doctor's secretary for an appointment. And it had still taken me three days to get hold of him. I was now more than hopeful of some answers.

'So tell me. Before we jump into any serious discussion, I would like to know a little more about you. How about . . .'

'Actually, doctor,' I cut him off, unsure of how to go about this. 'I . . . this may come as an unusual request,' I smiled. 'But I'm here to inquire about one of your patients.'

'I'm sorry?' the doctor said firmly, conveying that my request was not welcome.

'Uh . . . yes. I wanted to know about one of your patients whom I happened . . .'

'I'm sorry, Ms Pandey, but I cannot entertain such requests. This is . . .'

'But . . .'

'Please understand that there are rules. I cannot . . .'

'Doctor, I don't want details of the patient's personal life or his whereabouts or what he discloses in your sessions. I just want to know what the problem is.'

'Look, Ms Pandey, I am sure you may have some reason for contacting me. But unfortunately, I can't help you. I suggest you ask your questions to my patient directly in case your intention is to help him. But I cannot disclose any information to you.'

'Please at least try to understand . . .'

'Now unless you intend to pay me for the hour, I would request you to make way for the next patient and appreciate the fact that I am not billing you for your time here.'

And that was the end of my first visit to Harsh's psychiatrist. And I say first because there was a second . . .

31

149 days before the wedding

Dr Marwah's secretary was being difficult. Shouldn't a psychiatrist's right-hand be more patient? Well, I had called her an inexcusable number of times in the last two weeks but that still didn't justify her flared nostrils when I walked into the clinic.

I had carefully wrapped a scarf around my face and casually thrown another around my body to 'disguise' myself in case Harsh was around.

Just like the last time, I had white-lied at home about my visit here because there was just no need to involve my family in this quest.

The doctor sighed as I entered his cabin. He started reiterating that he couldn't share patient details, but this time I had a different game plan.

'Actually, doctor, I'm here for myself today.'

'Here for yourself, as in, you are here to consult me as a psychiatrist?'

'Absolutely.'

'Ms Pandey, to consult a professional for therapy you need to have a concrete reason. I hope to make it clear that this is by no means a way to get something else out of my sessions.'

I could tell that the doctor could see through my plan. Who wouldn't? But that said, I was not doing anything wrong.

'Doctor, I am a fat girl with a broken engagement, a set of nagging parents, a society that won't let me live in peace till I find a boy to marry and no boy to marry me. If I don't need therapy I don't know who else does!'

'Fair enough. So we have this cleared that you are genuinely here to consult me.'

'Yes.'

'All right then, let us begin.'

After this, he went through some forms that the secretary had made me fill. I had done this the last time as well but the doctor had shooed me away before we could start. Once we had gone over facts like I had no major health issues, physical or mental, that I had not consulted any other counsellor before, that there was no history of any major physical or mental illness in the family, we began our session.

'Ms Pandey, you seem to be a confident woman, so I would straight away like to ask if there is anything in particular you want to talk about. Or we could just have a general chat for today's session so I can get to know a bit more about you and your lifestyle.'

'Actually, doctor, I don't really think I need anything like medication or treatment for my problems. I'm not losing it or anything; I'm not retarded. I just think it would help to talk to someone about what I am facing.'

He flashed me a very you're-such-an-amateur smile. Had I said something stupid?

'You think people who come to psychiatrists or counsellors are all losing it?'

I shrugged my shoulders.

'I don't blame you. That's the first thing that comes to mind when one thinks of a psychiatrist. But let me tell you, the majority of my patients come here to just talk. Today's lifestyle is taking a toll on the new generation. Eleven-year-old children complain to me about depression, not even sure how to spell it. Mostly all they need is a lifestyle change and someone to talk to. Eighty per cent of all diseases today are psychosomatic—meaning, of the mind. So just because you are here, it does not mean that you are losing it or that you are retarded.'

'Thank you for clearing that.'

Although I was there to find ways to get to know Harsh's story, I was coaxed into a regular therapy session. Well, I was paying him for it. If in the bargain, life became a little easier for me to handle then why the hell not?

With surprising ease, I told Dr Marwah my story. I poured my heart out about my childhood, about getting fat, growing up as the odd one out, about never having any regular experience with the opposite sex. I knew I was supposed to incorporate Harsh and veer the conversation towards him, but I got so engrossed in talking about my life that I didn't even realize when the session was over. I was actually upset about having to stop talking. The hour had helped me vent and I was surprised at how it made me feel. These people are magicians. How do they get one to talk about the deepest issues of one's life in spite of being total strangers? Is that why it is easy? Because there is no fear of being judged?

Feeling much lighter than any diet had ever made me feel, I left the clinic after booking a follow-up appointment with the secretary, who was still as crotchety on seeing me.

The discovery of Harsh's problem was helping me deal with my own.

32

141 days before the wedding

My secret visits to Dr Marwah's clinic made me feel as if I were hiding some sort of addiction from my family. But this time I didn't lie about it, there was no need. I just took a few hours off from work and went to the clinic. It surprised me that more than learning about Harsh, I was looking forward to talking to Dr Marwah again.

After the initial courtesies, I dived right into my story, not at all conscious of how eager I must have seemed to start talking. I could tell that the doctor was happy with my enthusiasm and he put on his ever-so-ready-to-listen look as I launched into my story.

Fifteen minutes into the session, I was talking without any inhibitions, straight from the heart.

'I don't understand why society decides how something or someone should be. Man: broad shoulders.

Woman: small waist. Man: tall and muscular. Woman: fair and petite. Damn it! What if a woman is tall, dark and muscular? What if she doesn't have a small waist?' I said, punching my right fist into my left palm.

The doctor didn't flinch. I saw a hint of a smile play on his lips but otherwise he was in control. He was used to this.

'I'm sorry, doctor. I don't mean to be aggressive.'

'It's perfectly fine. Please continue.'

'I . . . I'm just so sick of this stereotyping. It gets tiring to constantly try and fit in. And the worst part is that I want to be part of the stereotype. I'm just so horrible. I hate thin girls. But I want to be a thin girl. Do I hate them because I am not one of them? What is my problem doctor? Even though I have accepted how I am why does it get so difficult to live with this image sometimes?'

Dr Marwah was about to say something but I had so much left to say. I had made a mental list, in fact. I had to cut him off.

'Doctor, why don't boys want to marry fat girls? Why do beautiful, thin, successful girls easily embrace the ugliest of boys with the roundest of potbellies but when it comes to fat girls there are no takers? I have had rishtas of divorcees and widowers. Not that I think of them as unworthy but you know what I mean? Is marrying me such a big compromise on the part of the groom's side? And to top that, I'm one engagement down now! I'll get grandfathers and criminals as options now,' I almost sobbed.

'And you know what the funniest part is? I'm not even so desperate to marry! Like . . . I couldn't care. I'm fine with my life. But since this topic has started, I've had no peace. I'm . . . I'm confused. I'm having an internal war of sorts.'

'Hmm. You've mentioned your broken engagement a couple of times. Tell me more about it,' the doctor said coolly.

And suddenly I was reminded of my motive. This was my cue. I had come here on a mission. The target had blurred a little, I had taken my eyes off the prize for just a little while, but it was time to kill two birds with one stone now. I hoped fervently that this would work.

'Doctor, among all the proposals—actually they weren't proposals, just meetings with families, you know how it is, the typical tea parties. So there was one family with whom matters actually progressed. Everybody else had refused. For some reason, this family agreed to meet me again. I was willing to go through with it for the simple reason that they had said 'yes'. Can you believe how low my self-esteem is? I don't know how to value myself, doctor. I was willing to marry him just because he hadn't said 'no' and because I was not sure if I'd ever find someone who would say 'yes'. I didn't even like him . . . But on the other hand, I didn't hate him. He's just the most absurd person I've ever come across,' I said, sensing a drum roll in my head.

'Do you want to know his name?'

'Not necessary,' Dr Marwah said, as if he were incapable of displaying curiosity. 'In fact, in my therapies we follow a code of anonymity. If that gets difficult, I let patients use fictitious names for people in their lives because it makes them less wary and more comfortable. So . . .'

'Okay, the name I want to use is Harsh . . . Harsh Tripathi,' I said looking straight into the doctor's kind eyes. For the first time, I had taken him by surprise. A look of recognition, of adding two and two together flashed across his face, as if to say, 'So you're the fat Madhurima he keeps talking about!' But within seconds, he had recovered his equilibrium. Somehow, I was sure that he had heard about me from Harsh and this fact made my heart dance a little. I was suddenly the girl about whom boys spoke to their therapists! Woohoo! Finally, I was getting some experience of what college life should've been like.

'Do you not like the name, doctor? Shall we go with, um, Harvinder Trivedi instead?'

'Harvinder Trivedi?'Dr Marwah smiled. 'Doesn't really go, does it?'

'Well, it is a *fictitious* name, so what does it matter?'

'I see what you're doing here, young lady.'

'What, doctor?' I smiled innocently.

He sighed.

'Come on, doc. You think everything I said was made up?'

'No, I know it comes from a place of real struggle. But . . .'

'Then hear me out.'

For the next few minutes, I narrated the whole episode with Harsh's family—his dominating mother, annoying sister, shrewd father and of course, the strange man himself, the engagement, the lack of romance, the car fiasco, the break-up, everything. I gave him all my insights into Harsh's personality hoping to complete the picture now. He knew one side of the story already, although I was not sure how much of it he knew. Giving him another point of view would help him evaluate Harsh's personality and solve his issues even though I didn't know what they were.

'So what do you think, doctor?' I asked after my detailed narration.

'About what in particular?'

'Um . . . about my fiancé. Ex-fiancé. From what I've told you, what do you *think* his problem is?' I asked, playing my card.

Dr Marwah played his part well, still reluctant to divulge any information. 'It's impossible to tell. The person you've just described may not have any problem at all or could be a complete mad man. I can't just guess like that.'

'Please, doctor,' I said in a small voice. He could do this for me. It was not directly a breach of his code of conduct.

'I think it doesn't matter what I think of the boy. We'd need more than just a double session to crack that. But what we need to be working on is you. Not somebody who is no longer a part of your life.'

'Don't you see, doctor? What you *know* . . . I mean . . . what you *think* could be his problem can really help me. It can help me understand him better. It can help me get closure. It can help me understand whether I was the problem between us or not. I need this from you, doctor.' I said emotionally. Could there be a better way to blackmail your doctor than promise him progress?

'Okay look. I get your point,' he said and paused. 'But I don't guarantee that this will help you. For all you know it may complicate matters further.'

'It won't. I promise.'

'Okay. Fair enough. You want to know what I *think* is your fiancé's problem is.'

He was not my fiancé but I couldn't disturb the doctor's flow. I nodded.

'I don't *think* he has any major problem to begin with. He *probably* suffers from an anxiety disorder that makes him socially awkward. Additionally, he *may* suffer from selective mutism that makes people tongue-tied in front of a particular audience and in this case, that audience *could be* people of the opposite gender. Often, such anxiety stems from a troubled childhood or after experiencing a harsh incident in adolescence. Sometimes, disorders are also genetic. But in this case, I *have a feeling* that it has just developed because of an awkward and shy boyhood. Nasty friends, unfriendly parents and discouraging teachers can destroy anybody and result in the development of anxiety, which otherwise would have been dormant. This disorder is not life-threatening to begin with but can greatly affect the daily lives of individuals. It should not be looked upon as a flaw but at the same time should not be taken lightly.'

Whoa! That was a lot to process. It took a few moments to catch up with the doctor and fully understand all that he had revealed.

The doctor had actually been kind enough to bend his rules a little. He had stepped out of his boundaries without technically stepping out of them. He had just revealed to me that Harsh had an anxiety disorder, a DISORDER! Such a heavy term and yet it was a relief to learn that Harsh wasn't suffering from something like depression or lunacy. Thank heavens! I didn't almost marry a psycho.

I wanted to thank the doctor for telling me all this but I had so many more questions. I wanted to know more. And thanking him would mean that I was done fishing out information from him. Well, I wasn't even close!

'You mentioned mutism. Selective mutism,' I asked and paused to form a question in my head. It was getting a bit shaky.

'How can one not be able to speak in front of women? A person must encounter several at any given point in their day. I mean his mother, his sister, his friends.'

'So you can imagine how difficult such a person's daily life must be. However, in front of women with whom this person has always been since childhood, anxiety may not exist or maybe subdued. Mother, sister, even cousins and maybe childhood girl friends. But with anyone other than that, especially someone he may be attracted to, someone his age, there is a problem.'

'It's . . . it's just so unbelievable,' I said, recalling my interactions with Harsh. Knowing that there was something so serious behind his behaviour changed my perception of him. You know how I always wanted a concrete cause, like a medical reason behind my sudden weight gain? Something that would justify my flaw, make them acceptable to the world. The doctor had done that for Harsh. He had justified Harsh's cryptic behaviour. And suddenly I was no longer frustrated with him. My anger, my confusion, my frustration, were replaced with sympathy.

'But I'm sure you know that Harsh had seen . . .'

'I don't *know* anything, dear,' Dr Marwah said carefully, with a smile.

'Yes, of course. I meant . . . *as I had mentioned*, Harsh had seen many girls before me for marriage and rejected all of them.' Even as I posed my query, I realized what the answer was.

'Who told you he rejected them? Did he?'

Of course! His mother had lied. He hadn't rejected any of them! They had all rejected him. Oh my god! Harsh was just another Madhurima! Tears pricked my eyes but I managed to stay composed. There was too much left to know.

'But what about the fact that he never even bothered to contact me after the break-up? I can understand his reservation, his lack of romance, but what about the fact that he supported his parents in blackmailing mine for the car? Which self-respecting man who can easily afford a car or two with his own money would do something like that, disorder or no disorder?'

'Did *you* contact him after the break-up? And are you absolutely certain that he knew that your parents were buying the car? Isn't there the slightest possibility that he didn't know?'

I recalled the discussion when Harsh was talking about the new car on our way to his cousin's wedding. His excitement was genuine, like an innocent child's. It was totally possible that he was in the dark about the arrangement between our fathers. Maybe his parents hadn't told him that my father was buying the car. Could it be that Harsh's parents were the villains in our story?

My discoveries had completely sobered me down, reducing my otherwise loud voice to a mere whisper.

'Yes, it could be possible,' I uttered as if trying to convince myself.

'But . . . but doctor . . . how can it work like this? Can such a person ever have a normal life? If he gets married, how will it work? I almost married him. You can't forever be nervous of speaking in front of your wife!'

'That is why people come to us,' Dr Marwah said, proud of his occupation. 'Harsh's problem is not . . . *doesn't seem like* a chronic one *from what you say.*'

I couldn't believe that we were still pretending not to be talking directly about his client.

'With time, it gets easier. He had been on dates with you, right? He *did* initiate conversation, however lacklustre it may have been.'

I scoffed.

'Well, I would hardly call those less-than-friendly meetings 'dates'. And initiate conversation? Please doctor! He would send me philosophical forwards that he sent to people first thing in the morning! Who does that?'

'And what if he did that just to start a conversation with you? What if he didn't send them to anybody else like you're assuming? Starting a conversation with a woman is not easy for many men, even those without anxiety disorders. Sometimes, the easiest things prove to be most difficult for some people.' It was as if he had stolen my thoughts, as if he had shown me a mirror. Who could know this better than I? I had struggled to do things that the world around me did with effortless ease.

'You're so right, doctor,' I said, almost in a stupor.

I thought of Harsh's morning messages. Yes, there was a pattern. Every morning, without fail, he would think of me at the same time. If it were indeed true that those messages were his attempts to talk to me, then I was touched. Suddenly, they assumed a new meaning, a romantic gesture.

I was discovering a new Harsh and one to whom I could relate.

'All right, I think it's time for us to wind up the session. I don't think you'll need a follow-up, now that I have given you all the information you need,' Dr Marwah grinned.

I smiled back. I wanted to go on talking, go on asking questions but I knew it was time to stop. The doctor had done enough for me and I had a lot to mull over.

'Before we conclude, I want you to think about this, consider my theory for a moment. You've mentioned several times how you've felt judged and been treated differently because of your weight and this has killed your confidence. How people always expect men and women to fit into certain stereotypes. Man: muscular and tall; woman: slim and petite. Right?'

'Yes, doctor.'

'I want you to dwell on the fact that there are more than just physical stereotypes.'

My brows creased automatically.

'Hear me out. You've complained that you've never had romance in your life. Have you ever initiated romance?'

How could I? I was 'the girl' I thought, defensively. And right there. Right there was the doctor's point!

'Uh . . . no.'

'Of course, initiating does not guarantee the blossoming of a romantic relationship. Let us forget about your school and college life. Consider your short stint with your fiancé. Did you ever initiate romance?'

Okay, this was beginning to make me feel terrible.

'I . . . I did initiate conversation.' That drunk-dialling incident instantly came to mind.

'Fair enough. Was there any reciprocation from the other end?'

'Uh . . . yes. But . . .'

'Just listen to me. I'm not bashing you or anything. I am trying to help you understand this better.'

'So, is it safe to say that whenever you initiated something you got a response?'

'Yes.'

'This means that there wasn't a lack of interest on the other side. Maybe just a lack of courage to initiate.'

'Well, if you put it like that . . .'

'Yes or no.'

'Maybe, yes.'

'So, why can't you be the one to initiate romance?'

'Because . . . because . . .'

'Because you've grown up with the notion that it's always the man who has to go down on his knee.'

'But . . .'

'It's completely understandable. You've labelled men as romantic just as people have labelled women as thin. But because you don't fit into that label, it pricks you. And because you are not a man you don't even see the ways in which you have generalized men.'

What was this sorcery the doctor was using to make me sound like a hypocrite? Of course, I was crying by now. But that didn't make the doctor stop. Mechanically, he offered me a few tissues from a box placed strategically between us. No consoling, no comforting. I was allowed to cry without being stopped.

'Stereotyping people is human nature. And that's not even the problem here. The problem is to be able to acknowledge the exceptions to the rules. It's important to validate them, to make them feel equal. Most women might be thin, but fat ones are also women. Most men might be macho and romantic and confident but the shy ones are also men. If the idea is to have romance then does it matter who initiated it?'

'It doesn't,' I sobbed, blowing unabashedly into the tissue.

'*Have you seen the excuse of a man that Harsh is? Do you really think I would be happy with an ugly loser like him?*'

My words came back to haunt me. How easily people like Harsh become losers for others! I have been on that side of the fence too and it has been rough. Harsh was not a loser. He was just grossly misunderstood. I dared to not even try to imagine what his struggle must have been like. People cannot even relate to such an issue, to such a problem, let alone understand and accept it. But I could. I could empathize with him. I could vouch that every little hardship he might have faced because of his anxiety disorder was valid even if nobody else in the world agreed.

Dr Marwah waited patiently for me to leave and I took my time doing so. I was suddenly feeling lost. Where did this leave me? I'd made the discovery. I'd unearthed a heap of reality. But, nothing had really changed. I had to go back home where the after-effects of a tragedy could still be felt at times. I didn't think I would be able to forget about all this anytime soon.

When I reached the threshold of the room, I turned and said, 'One last question, doctor.' Of course, he smiled. He always smiled. It must get tiring.

'What am I supposed to do now?' I asked, hoping he would give me some direction.

'It's not necessary for you to do anything,' he said and that is the last I heard from him . . . for a while.

33

135 days before the wedding

Don't judge me for trying to bump into Harsh outside his office for the third time in two days.

Yes, I had decided to seek him out but not for any particular reason. I just wanted one good meeting with him, maybe over a coffee, even though I wasn't sure why I wanted to see him. It had everything to do with my sessions at the psychiatrist's clinic. The term 'psychiatrist' no longer made me think automatically of mental asylums. Consulting one had made me realize that more often than not they're just professional listeners. The world needs more of them.

The discovery of Harsh's anxiety in front of women; the coincidence that he and I had never had romantic relationships in our lives; the fact that we were both somewhat in the same boat; that he was still trying to cope; the probability that no one in his life actually knew him; and, most of all, the truth that I had never initiated anything with him, with anyone rather, compelled me to do this: to seek him out.

The plan was to reach his office and then come up with a spontaneous plan of action. So that's what I attempted to do at first. Obviously, it was a terrible idea but I didn't know it then. I had waited outside his office the previous morning. I had reached early enough to avoid missing his entry into the building. But it took just three seconds of spotting him to send me packing, deciding never to do this again.

However, I bravely made a second attempt this morning, driven by the nagging need to correct something I hadn't really wronged. I wanted to tell Harsh, somehow, that I didn't think he was a loser. I had never really told him so, but I knew what rejection could do to a person— it could make you a loser in your own eyes. Maybe I needed to do this to clear my conscience. Maybe it was because I knew how it felt to be a misfit, to have no one understand your struggle. The reasons were plenty; the mission was one, but the agenda? I hadn't figured that one out.

On day two, I managed not to flee on seeing him. I was close to calling out his name but unfortunately, someone else called him at that moment and we couldn't meet. A rather upbeat fellow, this man who was probably Harsh's colleague, joined him outside the gate and the two chatted all the way up to the main office building, giving me no window of opportunity to intercept them casually.

As I watched the ease with which he conducted himself with his colleague, Harsh seemed like an altogether different man. No one could guess from afar that this smiling, jovial, backslapping man was socially challenged when it came to women.

In the last couple of days, I had done a little lay person's reading on selective mutism and anxiety. From what I read, it was more of a phobia than a disability but nothing one couldn't overcome with the right kind of support.

On this third attempt, I had better chances of success. I had abandoned the idea of calling out to him. I just planned to be standing in some obvious spot near the gate and hoped to be noticed—a first for me. It was a fool proof plan since it's not exactly difficult to spot me. This time I was hoping to 'bump into him' after work rather than before. Leaving my office about twenty minutes earlier, I made it over to his office in good time, definitely before he would be done. The only problem was that I had no idea how long I would have to hang around pretending to be passing by.

I could've just called, you know? If only people had more guts, there would be so many more love stories.

Calmly, I strolled outside the main gate as the evening blended into the night, cautiously peeping into the direction of the lobby for any signs of Harsh. I had seen him go inside in the morning so he had definitely made it to work. Unless he had left much earlier or there was another way out of the building, Harsh could not have missed my watch.

My feet started to hurt from all the standing and loitering as my wait stretched to an hour with still no sign of Harsh. Finally, I had to admit that this was extraordinarily stupid. Why was I making such a pointless effort? What was the need to pretend to meet him by chance—was I running away from taking the first step again?

No. *If I have to do it, I might as well do it right*—I gave myself a not-so-rubbish pep talk. I could just dial him, have a word, tell him that I was in the area and thought of catching up with him and it would totally not be weird. He would be too stumped to say anything, anyway. I was the stud between the two of us. There was nothing to be nervous about.

Taming my stray strands of hair in the side mirror of a random car, I took my cell phone out of my handbag. Why was I so anxious to contact a man who already had anxiety issues of his own?

I clicked on his contact number and the call button was bravely pressed. With every passing second, I got more and more nervous. Suddenly the first ring sounded—my cue to chicken out. But valiantly, I fought the urge to disconnect the line. The phone rang and rang and rang. Like a crescendo building up, I felt the ring progress to its natural end but right before the climax could turn into an anti-climax, Harsh picked up the call.

'Hello?' he said shakily, hesitation laced his voice.

'Hello,' I said, matching him tremble for tremble. We were two peas in a pod and now it was time to rewrite our story.

34

Umpteen days after the wedding

Today, it is a year since my wedding (to Harsh, in case you're wondering). Who would have thought? As I sit flipping through the wedding album on my lap, I can hardly believe how far Harsh and I have come in getting to know and love one another.

Our story has been nothing less than a dramatic movie, what with all the rejections the break-up, discovering secrets, the reconciliation and of course, the famous, inevitable War of the Parents. Where is the drama in your love story if at least one side of the family isn't dead against the wedding?

My second innings with Harsh began on a much better note than the first one. This time, I had taken it upon myself to change him or at least undo the damage I may have done by calling off our wedding version 1. To say that he was awkward when I randomly landed up

197

outside his office that day would be an understatement. But since he was awkward, he didn't ask too many questions, giving me the upper hand in over the situation. I pretended as if it was totally normal for people who break engagements to suddenly show up and ask their exes out for coffee. And you know what? By the end of that coffee, it actually started to feel a little normal. Once I stopped thinking about how absurd this date was, when I stopped trying to identify the purpose behind the meeting and, more importantly, when I started enjoying the coffee and the company, it stopped bothering me that this was awkward. I initiated the conversation and Harsh kept it up. It was really just that easy to begin again.

Then I decided to leave it at that. It's true that I was open to something brewing between us, for real this time, but that was not the reason to befriend him again. So after the first meeting, I didn't push for another, until about a week later when I woke up to one of Harsh's famous forwards. This time his generic message didn't irritate me. In fact, it made me smile because I knew the rationale behind it. He was thinking about me. He wanted to talk to me. This was his attempt to strike up a conversation and it was my turn to reciprocate. Harsh didn't know it yet but I had started to figure him out. I decided to ask him out for a movie in the evening. So what if I'm the girl in the story? *If the idea is to have romance then, does it matter who initiates it?*

On a side note, theatres are officially the best place to break the ice with socially awkward people. There's no need for small talk, there's no anxiety about keeping up the conversation, you can look like shit because it's too dark to notice anything, you basically have to do nothing for a couple of hours and still get to go home after a successful date. And the best part—the armrest effortlessly teaches you how to hold hands. It's as if you don't even have to try (okay, maybe a little) and from gawkily avoiding skin contact on the first date, you suddenly can't get enough of each other's fingers on the fourth. Man, we were going fast!

On our fifth date, I got an unexpected call from Mother thirty minutes after I had left home, asking me where I was.

'Are you sure you're with Anu?' she said, giving me another chance to tell her the truth but what was I supposed to do? Just change my story and say, 'No, I thought I was with Anu but turns out that the man sitting next to me in the theatre is actually Harsh.' Of course, I had to stick to my story of being with Anu, even though I could see that my game was up.

'Yes, mom. I'll be home soon,' I whispered.

'Oh, you'll be home right away! Because I was just in the market and happened to bump into Anu. And unless my old eyes are mistaken I didn't see you with her!'

Damn! Could Anu not have gone shopping for one day? By this time, she was officially separated from Akshay. They were taking a little time apart to decide what to do next.

You can imagine my plight at being caught red-handed by Mother. Telling them about Harsh after all the melodrama of the last few months could jeopardize the little thing that he and I had going. We weren't even sure what we were doing spending all that time together. Apart from figuring out things between us, I now also had to figure out what I would tell my family. This was obviously going to be a disaster. Suddenly I was steering everything around me. I was the one point of communication since Harsh was too busy being anxious, my parents were too busy being parents and his parents were . . . well, irrelevant at that point.

When I reached home, fully prepared to give them another cock-and-bull story about being called to the office for some urgent work, I was surprised by what happened next. Few minutes after I reached, the doorbell rang and, to my family's shock, it was Harsh.

What the hell was he doing? I knew how to handle the matter. This was not part of the plan. I gave an extra loud gasp on seeing him in order to show that I had no idea why he was at home.

'Harsh, what are you doing here, beta?' my mother asked firmly, balancing her kindness and animosity like a pro.

'Yes, what are you doing here?' I repeated quickly after her, trying my best to convey with my eyes that he needed to get the hell out but he totally ignored me.

'Uncle, aunty, I need to talk to you both about Madhurima and me.'

Madhurima . . . I liked that he used my full name. Not many did. And this was a totally inappropriate time to celebrate this fact.

Grandma was enjoying this little skit being played out in front of her. I could see in her eyes that she was looking forward to whatever was about to start, excited to lend her expert advice on the matter.

Avoiding my gaze completely, Harsh sat my parents down and began a conversation that was going to change my life forever. As he confidently launched into whatever it was that he was going to say, I felt like throwing up. I was not sure how my parents would take this. This was the same man they had wanted me to marry and after all that drama, I had been the one to call if off. And he was not even the main problem. The problem was his family. Things had got quite ugly between my parents and his towards the end of our first innings. Why was all this happening so fast?

'I know all this might come as a big surprise to you,' Harsh was saying. I was aware of the conversation only partially in all the panic. I retreated to the kitchen, too happy to flee the scene but I still heard the discussion in fragments.

'But, beta, after everything . . .' my father was saying.

'I'm confused,' my mother was saying.

Grandma was quiet. Harsh had stumped her. And this alone should have qualified him to marry me.

Some more jibber-jabber took place as I poured myself a glass of water but couldn't manage to drink it. In a way, I was grateful to Harsh for tackling the matter alone, but I just couldn't deal with the fact that this was happening. We could have planned how to do this. Why was it happening like this?

'With your blessings and if Madhurima agrees, I would like to marry her,' Harsh said smoothly, not an ounce of hesitation in his voice. Who was this man? And what had he done with the nervous wreck I knew?

Did Dr Marwah forget to mention that Harsh had an alter ego?

I decided to go back to the living room, nervous but eager to tackle the matter and to see everyone's reaction. And there Harsh was, confidently awaiting an answer from my parents. He'd never seemed this attractive to me and I'd never been this furious with him. Of all the opportunities he had had to be macho, he had to choose this one! As soon as I entered, Harsh flashed a smile at me, which conveyed a hundred emotions at once. (Finally, no more brotherly looks from him—yay!) Happiness, shyness, love, uncertainty, nervousness—that single moment contained everything. His anxious eyes seemed to be asking so many questions: Have I done the right thing? Are you happy with this? Do you love me too? Do you want to marry me too?

I could actually feel the colour rising in my face. This man had just asked for my hand in a room full of people. I felt giddy with excitement. There were butterflies in my stomach or it might have been hunger.

How could I not smile back? With a small nod, I let him know that he had done the right thing. That I was happy with this. That I loved him and I wanted to marry him. There were no formal proposals, no verbal confessions of love, in fact, no words at all. It was the single most beautiful moment of my life.

My parents asked him for some time to think over the matter—their polite way of asking him to leave so they could catch hold of me and give me a good talking to!

What happened next? More drama. When Harsh approached his parents, all hell broke loose. They rang up my parents and lectured them on how 'loose' their daughter was to be chasing their son after 'they had called the wedding off'. When did that happen? They said they would rather their son never marry than marry me and a hundred other things that clarified that they were not on board.

In turn, my parents took out their anger on me, telling me that keeping them in the dark had been absolutely wrong on my part and that they too weren't in favour of the marriage. How ironic! Just a few months ago, these two families had brought us together and now they wanted us apart.

Amid all the chaos, Harsh and I never got to celebrate the fact that he and I actually wanted to marry each other now, willingly. We were together. We were in love, fatness, disorders and family feuds notwithstanding.

For the next few weeks, both families underwent many emotional upheavals. Constant arguments, emotional blackmailing, days of not talking, lengthy explanations and sincere requests to cooperate took every ounce of determination that Harsh and I had to make this happen. I found it so funny that I was convincing my parents to let me marry a man who they had been convincing me to marry just a few months ago!

'Don't you remember what they made you go through? Don't you remember their greed? The way they wanted Papa to pay for everything, including the wedding?' my mother would remind me every day. But I knew that Harsh was not part of the 'they' she was referring to. In fact, he was shocked and embarrassed when I told him about the whole car episode.

Although my family was tense, Harsh's was beyond melodramatic. His mother had decided to go on an indefinite fast if he didn't give up his intention of marrying me. Knowing my almost-was and now, mother-in-law-to-be's penchant for drama for drama, I didn't expect anything less. And knowing Harsh's awkwardness with women, I didn't expect him to be able to deal with this. Reluctantly, I suggested that we let the matter cool down for the time being by pretending to agree to our parents' wishes and continue seeing each other on the sly.

There was something very exciting about the idea of having a secret affair, but Harsh didn't agree. We talked over the phone every day, but didn't meet.

Over a period of time, I was able to break my parents' resolve with the help of my grandmother. Once again, she had managed to surprise me by supporting our marriage. I knew my parents were more gullible than Harsh's but it would not have been possible without Grandma.

Eventually, Harsh suggested we get married without his parents' approval but my family and I didn't agree. I decided to make one final attempt to reconcile with the Tripathis with an unexpected visit to their house, fully prepared to ask for their forgiveness (even though the mistake had been theirs). But it was a futile attempt. At least my parents had been polite enough to accommodate Harsh for the few minutes that he had dropped in. His parents didn't extend to me the same courtesy. And that was the final nail in the coffin for me. I realized that Harsh and I deserved this with or without anyone else. We deserved this for ourselves. At least, we had the blessings of my family for moral support.

We decided to have a small, intimate wedding and invited only forty-four people. We planned everything in just a matter of a month and it was more than enough.

Society tells you that you need to have this big fat wedding in order to make your day memorable. Films and magazines tell you that you need to be thin, you need to be perfect for the best photographs. Parents tell you about traditions, friends tell you about trends, but no one tells you the most important thing—to be happy on your wedding day, no matter what goes wrong because something ALWAYS goes wrong. If you haven't enjoyed your wedding day in spite of the big budget, the gaudy decor, the endless guest list, the expensive clothes and the excessive food then what the hell have you done all that for? And you don't necessarily need any of it to make it the best friggin' day of your life!

The run-up to my wedding was nothing but enjoyable. After seeing Anu at her wedding, I had vowed to myself that if and when I got married I would not be a dramatic bride. I would enjoy every little thing no matter how stressful it might get. I took three whole weeks off from work. I personally planned everything, from the invitations to the food and decor, for no wedding planner could plan my big day better than I. Even though it was a simple wedding, there was a lot of work and it kept us on our toes. My mother designed my wedding lehenga herself and we didn't give a damn about the latest trend or the fact that I was fat. Many distant relatives had sent feelers of their displeasure over our 'rushed wedding' but we didn't give a damn about that either.

Two days before the wedding, my grandma decided to take me for a Brazilian wax. You know what that is? Well, I didn't! And when I found out, I locked myself in the bathroom but Grandma dragged me out and all the way to Kammo's Parlour (which was obviously owned by Kammo aunty). I don't know what I was dreading more—getting a Brazilian wax or getting a Brazilian with my Grandma! The operation was unsuccessful. I tricked Grandma by challenging her to get one first. Eventually, we came back after getting facials. Thank God!

On the morning of my wedding, I woke up with the mandatory pimple that has to appear on one's wedding day but there was no need to panic. Mine was graceful enough to be hidden completely by make-up. This was the day I was going to be a bride, Harsh's bride. And nothing could dull the sparkle.

I didn't even bother hiring a make-up artist and got my grandmother to do the job for me. It was time to reap the benefits of the gazillion magazines she had read. When

I got into the bridal outfit my mother had designed for me (let's be honest, it was an exact copy of what Kareena Kapoor had worn in *Kabhi Khushi Kabhi Gham*), I stood in front of the mirror and cried. One might think that I was upset because my stomach was sticking out a little (a lot) or because of the stretch marks on the sides of my waist, or due to a hundred other aspects about me that weren't perfect. But it wasn't that. I was crying because I was the most beautiful bride I had ever seen . . .

* * *

It doesn't sink in that a year has passed since I got married.

I've regained the weight I had lost during the dance classes. But it's okay, I've learnt to embrace it. There are days I wear fitted pants and high heels to work and Harsh tells me I'm looking beautiful and then there are days when I'm unwell, hairy and without any make-up and he still tells me I'm looking beautiful. That's the best part about loving someone for who they are and not how they look.

Harsh's mother is turning less intolerable every day but the same cannot be said about his sister. Is it too mean of me that I pray every night before bed? Oh, I forgot to mention this! Just before our wedding, Harsh's parents had a dramatic change of heart and, letting go of their egos, made it to the ceremony in the nick of time, total Hindi-film style. It was perfect and I was actually happy to see them. They still don't see eye to eye with my family but that's something we just have to ignore.

Mother and I need something to crib about in Harsh's family, right?

Guess what my parents gifted us on our anniversary? It's red and we're going for a long drive in it tomorrow!

It took a few months before Harsh opened up to me about his anxiety disorder, but I was in no hurry. The last one year has helped me to understand it better. As an adolescent, Harsh was phobic of interacting with people other than his family. Lack of communication with his parents and lack of knowledge on the subject had let his condition go undetected through his early years. He went to an all-boys school. Gradually, and left with no choice, he learned to cope but couldn't make and keep friends as easily as others around him. College life was even tougher. He could manage to talk to the boys but being around girls was challenging. Since his problem was not an obvious one, neither he nor anyone around him could point it out. He was dismissed as a reserved boy and no one, including him, read too much into his reclusive behaviour. Even though he had crushes, he couldn't approach them. Throughout college, he had no girlfriends, not even friends who were girls.

Many people thought he was gay and often teased him about it.

Once Harsh started working, he was often in situations where dealing with women was inevitable. That's when he started to realize that this was more than just shyness. His regular international travels helped him develop his personality, although the first few trips made him feel like a fish out of water. His parents were not informed enough to see or understand the matter.

When it was time to get married, overcoming his anxiety became more difficult because he couldn't discuss the problem—he didn't even know it existed! He dodged marriage as long as he could, but when he turned twenty-seven, his parents took him on a bride-hunting spree. He met some wonderful girls, much prettier than me, slimmer and more educated but couldn't strike up a single conversation with anyone. One of them thought he was deaf and mute.

His parents couldn't understand what the problem was every time he was rejected. Everything would go well in the preliminary tea parties. But the families would back out after the girls would meet Harsh by himself. Harsh's parents knew there was a dearth of marriageable boys from good families in the 'market' so they had no clue why it was so difficult for them to find a girl. Three years were spent in this process. On the sly, Harsh had started seeing a psychiatrist, Dr Marwah, whom he had got hold of on the internet.

Then one day, destiny (a matchmaker) arranged a meeting between his family and mine. I'm pretty sure that his family was not keen but when Harsh agreed to meet me again, his parents pounced on the opportunity. I guess a fat bride was better than no bride at all. Who would give them grandchildren otherwise, right?

It was less difficult for Harsh to survive a conversation with me than it had been with the others. Maybe because he was getting better, maybe because I didn't intimidate him like other girls, maybe because it was meant to be. I'm sure there are a number of reasons that made it happen the way it did, but I know for a fact that it was easier for him to deal with me because I was not perfect, my flaw (fat) was obvious, I didn't make him nervous and I was equally wary about being judged. We were in the same boat.

While a perfectly normal girl like me was always considered flawed because of body weight, a man with deep psychological issues was considered perfectly fine because he appeared to be so. So absurd, isn't it? If our minds had bodies then people's take on what's beautiful and healthy would be totally different, wouldn't it?

In a way, Harsh's anxiety in front of women is a blessing for me (ha ha). If we go to a mall and there happens to be a hot girl wearing hot shorts, it's I who end up checking her out more than my husband! We're two little oddballs who've somehow ended up together and it's perfect.

Believe it or not, we spent our wedding night playing cards. Yes, playing cards! I think he was more nervous than I. We were able to consummate our marriage only on the last day of our honeymoon (yes, he's not impotent after all—hurray!).

In case you're wondering about that drunken phone call, I eventually discovered what had happened between us that night. It was the time when we were expecting the Tripathis to get back to us with an answer after the coffee date, almost convinced that it was a 'no'. Emboldened by all the alcohol at Anu's cocktail party, I had called Harsh up and fired him for not responding positively, stating that I was completely worthy of any man in the world. I'm sure Harsh has exaggerated but I have given him the benefit of the doubt. Just as I was scared of being rejected, Harsh too harboured similar fears. He didn't give his parents a green signal because he was positive that it would be a 'no' from me after that evening at Coffee & Co. He was actually shocked and thrilled to know that I wanted him to say 'yes'. He called me back to say he was going to tell his parents that he wanted to marry me but cut the call as soon as I answered and spoke to his parents directly. The rest is history.

Grandma is not too well these days. She wants to go on a cruise before she dies. Wants to try bungee jumping as well. Mother is dealing with her. Father watches Madhuri Dixit movies all day. Did I mention he is her most ardent fan? From buying her movie tickets in advance to selling them in black, he had done it all during his college days. From her autographs to photographs, he had everything. Grandma said he used to have a sexy poster of her in his bedroom, which Mother took down after marriage. Their wedding photograph hangs there now.

In fact, for the first few years after I was born, Mother didn't realize that my name was a tribute to the actress. Father had smartly roped in Mother's name and made it sound like an extended version of her—Rima's daughter Madhurima. Mother was touched by the suggestion. And then a few years later, while filling up my play school form, she stumbled upon the existence of Madhuri in my name. She confronted Father. As a consolation, they went on a holiday to Dubai.

Mother is fed up with Father's returning obsession but she is dealing with him as well.

Anu and Akshay eventually divorced a little after their first anniversary. She took up a job after her divorce and fell in love with a colleague. They are getting married next month.

Her first wedding may have looked like a fairy tale but I think it is her second marriage that will truly be the one. I've never seen her this happy, not even during her initial months with Akshay. We often joke that our kids will fall in love and get married to each other someday.

When I look back at how jealous I was when she first got married, I feel silly and juvenile. I've come to realize that people are not perfect but relationships can be. It's not perfect people, but perfect relationships that make fairy tales; and I cherish mine every day.

Epilogue

12 days before the wedding

'Remember, Madhu, the art is more important than the appearance.'

Grandma was in my room, imparting knowledge on the 'art of lovemaking' while I sat opposite her ready to throw up.

'You need something like this for your wedding night,' she said with evident mischief and excitement in her eyes. She was holding out an issue of *Vogue*, pointing at the picture of a top model, with obviously augmented assets, flaunting a racy red bikini, from the latest swimwear collection of a popular brand. I wanted to laugh and cringe with embarrassment at the same time. Do you know how funny and awkward it is when your almost eighty-year-old grandma walks into your room wearing a cervical collar and tells you what lingerie to wear on your wedding night?

'Nani!!!' I scolded her.

'What?' she asked, not willing to understand how weird this was.

'You're embarrassing me now.'

'Oh, don't be silly.'

A pause.

'Your mother is useless. She won't tell you all this. But remember, if a man is happy in bed he is happy in life.'

'Oh please, Nani! Men nowadays are different. There is more to life than just that.'

'Oh, you poor little naive girl!' she scoffed. 'Anyway, I'm not here to prove how much men love to diddle. It is just a word of advice I can offer. I don't have anything else to give anyway.'

Another pause.

'Take my advice. Don't jump into motherhood. Enjoy the first few years with your husband. These are the years in which you build the foundation of your marriage. Be outgoing, be experimental; have fun. Don't make yourself a trophy wife. Keep working.'

'Yes, Nani.'

'Your mother could have done wonders if she hadn't given up her job after you were born. She was very talented. You don't do that. You have the support, the will and the qualifications.'

'Yes, Nani.'

'And don't be a nun in bed.'

'Yes, Nani.'

'Remember, a man only steps out of his marriage for lust. It may seem like love, but initially it is always lust, which over a period of time takes the shape of love.'

'Yes, Nani.'

'And most importantly, love and respect everyone in your new house.'

'Yes, Nani . . .'

'Now should I order this red bikini?' . . .